Get A FREE Ebook!

Would you like a FREE ebook? JOIN Michele's newsletter to receive information about new releases, giveaways, and special promotions! To say thank you, I'll send you a FREE copy of The Inn at Pelican Beach. Sign up today!

https://dl.bookfunnel.com/wr9wvokoin

Chapter 1

Meg

"Cove Resort, this is Meg Carter speaking," she called out to her speakerphone while glaring at the ocean's continuous hues of blue. The alarm-like ring of the telephone always rattled off at the worst time, usually when she needed to focus the most. Something Meg certainly didn't miss when she worked from home.

The morning had already been long, and with a one o'clock meeting looming over her head, she hoped her new assistant, Anne, would handle the phone calls.

"Meg, I'm so sorry to bother you. I know you're trying to prepare your slides. But there's a gentleman in the front lobby by the name of Parker who's eagerly requesting to see you. I would imagine he's someone you know?" Anne's voice tapered.

Meg glanced at her digital watch, confirming absolutely nothing. *Hmm.* "Are you sure he's here at the resort?"

"Yep. He's downstairs. Would you like for me to tell the front desk to send him up? Or —"

Meg shifted in her chair, as if that could mask the feeling of her lower stomach fluttering uncontrollably. She then slid into her heels. "No. I'll go down. If you can just cover the phones for me, I'll be back in ten to fifteen minutes tops. If I don't finish getting the rest of this presentation together, Iris is going to chew me up and spit me out for lunch," she said.

"Iris Knowles — the regional boss. Big-wig, head-honcho, stuffy type, right?"

Although she'd only been on the job for a short time, Anne had a way of mentally computing names, profiles, and personalities. A good quality in Meg's eyes, as long as she didn't slip up and mistakenly misuse her superpower at the wrong time.

"Right. Oh, and Anne, if she calls, please forward her to my cell. The last thing I need is to upset the woman while she's on her way over here. The meeting will be sabotaged before it gets started, and that's a risk neither the directors nor myself are willing to take."

In a robotic voice, Anne replied. "Forward head-honcho to Meg's cell. Got it."

"Thanks, Anne."

Meg bit her bottom lip while disconnecting the call. She then shoved the cellphone in her pocket, reapplied her favorite lipstick, and was out the door, leaving nothing but the echoing sound of her heels trailing behind.

On the ride down the elevator, she considered, *it's healthy to take breaks, right?* Especially when those breaks involved seeing Parker Wilson.

Before she could lift her red toes in three-inch sandals off the elevator, she heard that deep, familiar, captivating voice echoing across the hall. It was him, alright. Her crush, her heartbeat, her guy standing with a paper bag in hand while entertaining an elderly couple. Technically, it wasn't official. He wasn't really her guy. But, they'd been spending a lot of time together, growing more fond of one another. *Falling more deeply in —*

"Parker?" she said.

His eyes locked with hers. "There she is. I was just talking about you. Meg, meet Mr. and Mrs. Malloy. This fine couple is celebrating their fortieth wedding anniversary right here at the resort. Forty years and they're still going strong. Isn't that something?"

Meg extended a warm smile to the couple. "It is. Happy anniversary."

Mr. Malloy reared back with a hearty chuckle. "I like to tell people you don't get that much time for robbing a bank."

His wife rolled her eyes. "You'll have to forgive my husband. He spent over thirty years in law enforcement and still can't stop making connections to the old job."

"Ah, law enforcement... bank robberies. That makes sense," Meg replied. "Well, it brings me a lot of joy to meet couples such as yourself. I'm hearing more and more about people going their separate ways, so your story is particularly encouraging."

Parker reached over, gliding his hand across her back. "I'd like to think there are still plenty of couples who believe in love and are still going strong. Don't you?"

His words resonated with Meg. It was a far cry from what she'd experienced with her ex, John. He was so-called head over heels in love when he proposed. Then he somehow fell out of love, met another woman, and broke off their engagement, only to crawl back months later, begging for her forgiveness. *Really?*

Meg smiled. "I'm sure of it. And in the spirit of love, Mr. and Mrs. Malloy, it would bring the staff here at the resort such great pleasure to do something fun for your anniversary. How about you enjoy a complimentary dinner at the resort? I'll speak to the front desk and ask them to set up the reservation for you right on the grounds. What do you say?"

Mrs. Malloy clasped her hands over her mouth. "Oh, how

generous of you. We would love to enjoy a complimentary meal, wouldn't we, Honey?"

"Yes, dear." Mr. Malloy then leaned in closer, whispering to Meg, "We're staying in room 2 1 7, in case the front desk asks for our information. My wife enjoys fine dining, so any opportunity for me to save a buck or two is greatly appreciated."

Again, his wife rolled her eyes. "I'm not deaf, Malloy. I'm standing right here and can hear every word you're saying. Now, let's give these two a minute to themselves, please. I have an appointment at the spa that I don't want to miss. Young man, what was your name again?"

"Parker."

She nodded. "Yes, that's right. Parker, it looks like you have a good woman on your hands. Just remember to always treat her like a queen. Spare no expense for the one you love."

Mr. Malloy wore a devilish smile plastered across his face as he cleared his throat. "Excuse me. Carry on."

Parker smiled. "I'll have to keep that in mind, Mrs. Malloy. It was nice meeting you."

Once the couple drifted away, disappearing into the crowd in the lobby, Meg returned her attention toward the paper bag. Casually interlocking fingers, she said, "What a surprise. I didn't expect to see you here today."

He raised the bag, placing it in her hands. "It's your favorite. Conch salad from Terry's stand. I had this feeling you were working nonstop, so I figured I'd stop by and bring you something."

She closed her eyes for a second, inhaling the contents of the bag. "Parker, you know me too well. I'm starving. Not only did I skip lunch, but I'm under pressure to tie up loose ends for a meeting I have coming up in less than —" She paused, glancing down at her watch. "Crap. I'm sorry. I hate to run, but I really need to go."

The pressure didn't stop her mind from wandering, noticing his outfit, and how particularly scrumptious he looked. She'd give anything to throw caution to the wind, renting a boat for the afternoon and go sailing together, instead of being in a stuffy meeting.

Parker slid his hand alongside her arm. "No need to apologize. I expected you'd be busy. I just wanted to make sure you were taking care of yourself, that's all. After you recharge with a little lunch, you can press through the rest of the day, and then tomorrow you'll be working from home. You got this."

She paused, then leaned in, planting an unexpected, yet sweet, kiss. One that he returned wholeheartedly. "Parker, you need to go before I get in trouble." She smiled in between kisses.

The sound of heels approaching grew like a clanging cymbal interrupting a sweet symphony. The sound was followed by a stern woman's voice. "Trouble would be an understatement. Smooching in the front lobby while on the clock, giving away free meals just because it's someone's anniversary. Have you lost your mind?"

The woman behind the boisterous voice towered beside them, practically spraying them with saliva as she spoke.

Meg stammered. "Iris. I — I didn't see you standing there."

"That's obvious. I, on the other hand, have been around long enough to hear quite an earful."

Parker protested. "Ma'am, it's my fault. I just dropped by to —"

"Save it. Instead of standing here, giving you lip service, and putting on a full show for our guests, she should be upstairs doing her job. Last time I checked, we have a meeting, one that better knock the socks off not only myself, but our board members. If not, you'll have me to answer to."

Parker continued. "Ma'am, respectfully —"

By then Meg had slipped her hand over his. "Parker, it's okay. Thank you again for the salad. I have to go. We'll talk later, okay?"

Meg's pulse raced in a frantic way, watching as he silently retreated. On the inside, she knew what he was thinking. This woman was as much of a beast as she'd described. *Was she miserable... or perhaps lonely?* She wasn't sure. But whatever it was, Meg knew it wasn't good.

Chapter 2

Frankie

Frankie Jones pushed her rolling cart, stacked with employee benefit packets, through the lobby of the resort. Day one of processing new hires was behind her, leaving her wanting nothing more than to have a minute to herself.

Maybe she'd call her roomie, Meg, down in the sales department to make plans for later on. Or maybe she'd go back to the office and sit in silence for five minutes straight. Either way, her role as benefits coordinator had temporarily depleted her energy, which she usually didn't mind. But later tonight, she'd definitely need a breather.

"Hold the elevator." Frankie waved.

She cordially maneuvered past the guests, inhaling the scent of sunbathing products while landing her eyes on a gentleman holding the door. "Thank you," she exhaled.

Frankie pushed forward, thumping over the threshold of the elevator as the gentleman assisted with her cart.

Letting out an effortless sigh, she relaxed. "Thanks for your help. Walking around with this double-decker is no simple task."

"I can tell. It looks like you have quite the load." He extended his hand, noticeably locking eyes longer than one normally would. "I'm Christian, by the way. What floor are you going to?"

Frankie's morning was shaping up to be just as ordinary as most mornings. The checklist usually included eight a.m. emails, returning missed calls, and on special days, running rosters to help her keep track of new hire benefits versus current employees. Occasionally, she'd assist the director with other tasks and looked forward to spontaneous excursions around the resort.

Immediately noticing his crisp golf attire, fit waistline. and well-groomed beard, she answered, "The fifth floor, please. I'm Frankie. Frankie Jones." While displaying her best professional smile, she motioned toward the cart. "I'm the benefits coordinator for the resort."

"Ah, that explains the mounds of packets and brochures. Not exactly the kind of thing people carry around with them on vacation," he said.

Agreeing in laughter, she replied, "No fooling. If I had to carry this around on vacation, I'd cancel the trip."

It was then that she caught herself envisioning the idea. *A trip would be nice right about now. I could lie out in the sun with a fruity beverage and even have a hot guy like yourself by my side as an added bonus.* She glanced at him one more time. *Oh, who are we kidding?*

"Are you enjoying your stay here at the resort?" she asked.

"Somewhat. This is a business trip for me with an extended stay, if you will. The plan is to enjoy the surroundings as much as I can in between work," he explained, rocking back and forth from his heels to his toes.

"Smart plan. If you don't mind me asking, what do you do?"

The elevator bounced slightly, making a sound that resembled metal rubbing together, and then the lights flickered, followed by an abrupt halt.

She swallowed, staring ahead at the dim gray elevator walls while gripping the side rail. Unfortunately, that didn't make her feel any better. "Did we just stop?" Frankie asked.

Retorting with somewhat of a snarky remark, he said, "Yep. We're definitely not moving, that's for sure. Just my luck on a day where I have very little time to spare," he said, glancing down at his watch. "I have a conference call that begins in ten minutes, so we definitely need to get this baby moving."

Frankie cocked her head upward, barely glimpsing how calm and collected he was out of her peripheral. "This can't be happening. Come on elevator. Keep it movin'."

While feeling like the walls were starting to cave in, she recalled something she'd once seen in a movie. Frankie lunged forward, pounding her fist on the double doors. "Somebody help! We're stuck in there! Please, help us!" she yelled.

That's when it hit her. It wasn't just the movies that inspired her sense of panic, it was old fears she thought she'd conquered that came rushing over her like a tsunami.

A hand gripped her arm, gently pulling her back. "I'm not sure that's going to do you any good. Besides, if anybody should be yelling, don't you think it should be me? I'm the one with a meeting, remember? And, believe me when I tell you, my boss will rip me a new one for missing the call. So, why don't we try and stay calm together?" He took a short breath, then continued. "Now, fortunately, there's this little thing called an emergency call button. See, it's right here. All you have to do is press it."

She watched as he pointed toward the button, and somehow her fear slowly transitioned to anger over the demonstration fit for a child. "Well, since you're so familiar with how this works, why don't you go ahead and mash the button? Just do me a favor, please talk to me about remaining calm. I don't do small spaces," she said, wiping the sweat beads forming above her upper lip. "Being trapped in an enclosed environment is not exactly my cup of tea."

He nodded. "Understood. How about we swap places so I can try and get in touch with somebody? I'm sure whatever it is will be fixed in no time."

"Fixed?" she asked, promptly thinking it was a dumb question. In her mind there was a simple elevator reset button somewhere just waiting to be pressed, leaving no need to overcomplicate things.

He responded. "Yes. But don't worry about it. These kinds of things happen all the time."

She half listened as he babbled on the line with the securities operator. Technically, she didn't care what the issue was. She just wanted out. Ideally, she, as the employee, should be just as poised, cool, and collected as he was, but she couldn't be. All she could envision was the expression on her ex-husband's face the day he discovered her hiding from him in the guest bedroom closet. It was a little smaller than the size of the elevator, but much darker. She couldn't recall much from that night except for being knocked around a little and sitting in the dark crying afterward. To make matters worse, they hadn't even been married that long. She initiated an annulment after only six months. But when you join worlds with someone who was a professional by day and an unpredictable alcoholic by night, that was enough to make you hide in a closet. In her case, it was enough to send her packing. For good.

"What did they say?" she asked.

"They're working on it. Apparently, both elevators are

inoperable and they're calling the fire department as we speak. This is not exactly a good look for the resort, but I'm sure they'll do whatever they can to get us out of here."

Frankie slid down the back wall of the elevator, reaching for a brochure to fan herself with as she sat on the floor. "I owe you an apology. I snapped under pressure. As a member of the staff, I should be the one consoling you. Not the other way around."

His shoulders slumped forward as he joined her, side by side. "No need to apologize. I was being a jerk. My mind was so focused on my meeting, I nearly missed that you were having a —"

She nodded. "You can say it. It was a full-blown meltdown. Maybe even a panic attack."

"Hey, in your defense, elevators have a way of making you feel claustrophobic. The real question is, are you okay?"

She cracked a one-sided smile. "I'll be fine. Honestly, I don't know what triggered me in the first place." *That's a lie. You know exactly what triggered you,* she thought. But even if she knew, she wasn't about to share it with a complete stranger. "I guess at this point all we can do is wait it out."

Christian swiped the screen on his phone a few times, then laid it down. "Waiting is a lost art nowadays." He pointed to his cell. "Probably because of devices like these, among other things. Speaking of which, I don't have reception so I won't be calling the boss or anyone else for that matter. Guess that leaves us plenty of time to talk."

Frankie could feel his eyes on her as he spoke.

He folded his hands together. "So, Miss Frankie Jones. How long have you been working here at The Cove?"

"A little over two years. It's been a pretty neat experience, actually. Well, at least it had been up until now," she said.

"Oh, come onnn. You're not going to allow a small mishap like this to ruin your view of the job, are you?"

Her eyebrows folded like an accordion. "I don't suppose I will, but is this the same guy who was just frustrated minutes ago about getting out of here to catch a conference call? What happened?"

"Hey, there's no point in dwelling on it now. As much as I travel with the job, something like this was bound to happen anyway. Now, come on. Tell me all the good stuff. What's it like working behind the scenes at a five-star resort? I want to hear everything from an employee's perspective."

Frankie stretched out her legs, crossing one over the other. "What are you, some sort of reporter or something? Digging for information?" She chuckled.

"No."

"Okayyy. Well, if you must know, I'll start with the job. Working in HR is amazing. I get to interact with a lot of people. I even met my roommate by working in the department, so the job definitely has its perks. But, by far the most exciting part has been interacting with the guests when I get a chance and stealing away to enjoy the beach. If I had it my way, I'd live out there all day, every day."

In a high-pitched tone he asked, "Every day?"

"Yes. Especially here at the resort. Wait a minute. Don't think for one minute I don't recognize that you're trying to get my mind off this elevator situation."

He smiled. "Is it working?"

"Maybe."

Christian nudged her arm. "Good. Then don't fight it. Continue telling me what's so great about this place."

She thought about putting up a little more resistance, but what the heck? He was right. It's not like they had the freedom to get up and leave. "What's not to love? We have The Sand

Bar where I like to order my favorite strawberry daiquiris. Alcohol free, of course. I can't drink on the job. Then there's walking along the shore and chasing the waves… my absolute favorite way to relax. Then there's a little secret spot that I won't reveal, but serves as an excellent place to get away and unwind," she explained.

"A secret spot? Do tell."

"No way. A girl never gives up her secrets. All I can say is it's one of the most romantic hideaways the resort has to offer. A place where staff occasionally sneak away to unwind, and a place where the few lovers who discover it go for long walks to rekindle some of that magic."

Meg could feel a warm sense of curiosity and intrigue as Christian stared. But his next reaction, slowly clapping his hands, and then picking up the tempo, took her by surprise.

With a grin smeared across his face, he said. "Bravo. You just painted an amazing picture of the resort. But it sounds as if I've chosen to stay at a place that's really meant for couples and not single people like myself. Outside of drinking alone at the bar, what are bachelors supposed to do? Folks like us spend a ton of money on vacation to have nice accommodations only for the places to cater to couples and families more. I don't get it. No offense toward the resort and all, but it is an observation."

She raised her eyebrow. "Don't take this the wrong way, but don't you think the onus is on you? Keep in mind this is coming from a girl who knows what it's like to constantly have to do things on her own. But, that's not the resort's fault. I'm sure there are ways you can turn your experience around. For example, how many days did you say you were visiting?"

"I didn't say." He chuckled. "But since you're asking, I'll be here for about a week, and then I'll be moving on to another location in the area."

"Why don't you give yourself a little challenge? Be intentional during the next few days to get out of your room and go exploring a little. Who knows? You may actually meet someone who intrigues you enough to invite to dinner." *Am I really giving this man advice on how to find a date? I can't even find a date for myself, let alone help him.*

Her eyes met his long enough to feel awkward, forcing her to stutter. "Anyway, what I really meant to say is we definitely don't have a shortage of things to do."

He smiled. "That's great. Sounds like you'd be the perfect tour guide during my stay. When are you free to get started?"

"Me?" she asked.

* * *

Their conversation was interrupted by another round of flickering lights, followed by complete darkness. That coupled with a man's voice echoing from a floor below was enough to put Frankie's nerves back on edge. "How are you doing up there?" the voice called.

Frankie squeezed her eyelids shut. "We'd be a lot better if you could get us out of here, sir. This is Frankie Jones, benefits department from HR, by the way."

"Ms. Jones, this is the senior securities operator. We're working in conjunction with the fire department and will have you up and running very soon. Just try to remain calm."

Frankie spoke an octave above a whisper. "Trying to remain calm is easier said than done when you're stuck in a dark elevator with a stranger."

The lights flickered again, this time returning to their usual cadence. But it was Christian's gentle stare that caught her off guard. "Hey, I'm no longer a stranger to you. I'm the guy you were just laughing with. The guy you were about to tell off for assuming there was nothing for single people to do at the resort, remember?"

She released her clinch and cracked a smile. "Yes, I remember."

"Good. Because I'm also the same guy you're taking on a tour over the next several days of my stay. I'm going to hold you to it once we get out of here."

Frankie reared her head back. "Why me?"

"I can't think of a better person for the job. You know this place much better than I do. And —"

The elevator's motor cranked on, then began moving upward toward the fifth floor as if nothing had happened.

Frankie leapt to her feet. "We're moving!"

Without thinking, she turned and hugged Christian, who was also rising to his feet, gripping him for what felt like a full minute. "Ooh. I'm sorry, I didn't mean to —" She cleared her throat. "I'm just happy we're moving, that's all," she explained, hastily checking for her make-up on his shoulder blade as if somehow that would change the awkward moment.

One side of Christian's mouth rose slightly, exposing the sweetest dimple. "Don't apologize. I was secretly nervous the whole time and needed a hug."

Frankie blurted out in laughter. "Oh, stop it. You were cool as a cucumber the entire time, helping me to hold on to my sanity."

The bell sounded, alerting them they'd arrived on the fifth floor. Frankie adjusted her own clothing just in time for the doors to open.

With the entire department waiting to greet her, she dragged the cart outside the elevator, turning around at the sound of Christian calling her name. "Miss Jones."

"Yes," she said, looking up.

"You can find me in room 112 should you decide to change

your mind about the tour. I'd really enjoy your company," he said.

Standing speechless, she watched as Christian waved. Then the doors closed between them.

Room one-twelve? If that's where he's staying, then why did he ride past the first floor?

Chapter 3

Parker

"Chuck, my man. How's it going?" Parker rested his palm against his truck while taking in the views of his nearly completed beach house.

He'd accomplished so much with this particular live-in renovation, including meeting the woman of his dreams.

"Parker. All is well, my friend. Things are going to be even better when I tell you about this sweet deal that just came my way."

Parker had befriended Chuck Nesbit not long after moving to the island. As the man in charge of bank-owned properties, he was reliable for tipping him off every now and again to good deals and potential opportunities for renovation. "Really? I like the sound of that. Whatcha got for me?"

"Man, I hope you're sitting down because this one is a doozy, and undoubtedly the biggest project I've ever sent your way. It's guaranteed to push your net worth in the high millions if you think you can swing it. Notice I said high millions, with an s," Chuck emphasized.

"Nesbit, quit teasing me. What is it, a big-name resort?"

"No, I know you better than to expect that you would take on a resort. But how about a bed-and-breakfast right off the beach at Seaside Point?" Chuck asked.

Parker broke a long moment of silence, letting out a sigh. "Okay, basically a larger house with a few rooms, maybe four or five to be exact, plus a kitchen, I would presume, and what? An outdoor space for guests to go to the beach? I can renovate something like that."

The enthusiasm in Chuck's voice escalated. "Try a six bedroom with everything you mentioned and more. And that's just one property. There's also a second bed-and-breakfast of equal size, just a few doors down, plus a gift shop connected to this deal."

Parker walked toward the front porch, pausing at the last bit of information. "That's impossible. All the bed-and-break-fast properties are fully booked and operational at Seaside. There isn't a short sale or foreclosure on the strip for miles. Somebody must've given you some bogus information."

Chuck laughed. "This isn't a foreclosure, Parker. Have you heard of the guy that everyone refers to as Old Man Barnes?"

Parker nodded. "Vaguely. I've heard his name a time or two from the locals. Something about him being a wealthy loner who hires staff to run his late wife's business. That's all I know."

A grunt came from the other end of the line. "All I want to know is how much of a cut you are going to share with me once you make this deal. Apparently, the old man knows you better than you know him. My realtor connection tells me he's contem-plating a short sale. It seems as if he's been in over his head for a while now. But first he wants to speak with you. Between his health issues and not being able to keep up with the business like he once used to, I hear he's looking for a way out."

Parker unlocked the front door, marveling over the open floor plan and the panoramic view of the beach out back. The smell of fresh paint coupled with staged beach furniture waiting to be unwrapped was enough to make him want to stay forever. "Chuck, while I appreciate you trying to secure my financial future... correction, our financial future, I think this one might be over my head. I normally occupy one property, renovate, then sell to keep things clean and simple. This deal sounds like it has way too many strings attached."

"Parker, you haven't even heard the ins and outs of the proposal yet. Do me a favor. I'm going to send you Mr. Barnes' address and telephone number. All I ask is you go over and talk to him. If you don't like what he has to say, then you can tell him thanks, but the deal is not for you."

"Chuck, I already know the deal is not—"

"Parker. Hear me out, bud."

Parker placed his cell phone on speaker, freeing himself to wander about. "I'm listening."

"I was going to let you find out for yourself because he asked me not to go into detail, but the man called and spoke to me personally. Right now, he's interested in hearing from you, and I kinda gave him my word that you'd call him by the end of the day."

"Why did you do that?" Parker asked.

"Imagine spending the amount of money you did on your current renovation, but getting triple the return. If I were you, I wouldn't mess this up. Go and hear what the man has to say, or at least give him a call first."

A long streak of silence pierced the line before Parker spoke.

"Fine. Text me his information and I'll give him a call. But in return, I want a list of potential properties to visit. It's the least you can do for putting me in this position without my consent."

Laughter broke out on the other end of the line. "Somehow, I don't think you'll be needing another list from me, but I'll look into it just the same. Oh, and Parker, one more thing."

A groan from the depths of Parker's belly emerged. "What now, Chuck?"

"You and I have been close business partners, and I'd like to think buddies for a while now..."

Parker agreed. "And?"

"And — I'd like to think that means I know a thing or two about you. Now, it might be a stretch, but promise me you'll be open-minded and willing to consider something new. This could be life-changing for you."

"Chuck, don't do that to me. Is there something you know that I don't?"

A beep signaled the call had come to an end.

Great. Jussst great. Parker frowned at the screen. *By the way, Chuck, I was going to invite you to my pool party to celebrate the completion of the house this weekend, but I guess you're too busy to stay on the line long enough to hear about it —*

Parker pushed the phone to the side, feeling somewhat frustrated, yet intrigued, to hear what old man Barnes had to say.

* * *

Parker's eyes snapped open, realizing he'd dozed off in the new Adirondack chair. As if there weren't enough chores to keep him busy. Light fixtures still needed to be installed upstairs along with hardware on the doors. Miguel would stop by and polish a few things off the list. He'd celebrate, and that was it. In one, maybe two weeks max, Parker would have the for sale sign up, ready to reap the benefits of his hard work.

A quick glance at his phone revealed a message from Chuck. For now, it would have to take a backseat to the sound of the doorbell.

He stumbled, grabbing a t-shirt and swishing his hair in place. Swinging the front door open to the sight of a gorgeous hour-glass figure was enough to put him into a daze. Even on her worst day, he thought Meg was stunning. If only her eyes weren't filled with tears, he'd pick her up and swoop her around like he'd been accustomed to doing. "Meg, what's wrong?"

"I'm just frustrated, that's all," she groaned. "Maybe angry would be a more appropriate way to describe my feelings regarding Iris."

He opened up, welcoming her to rest in his arms. "I take it the meeting didn't go so well?"

"Parker, I'm all for taking responsibility for my own actions. She was right. To be downstairs smooching in the lobby was completely irresponsible. I get it. But I'm not sorry for giving that couple a complimentary dinner, and I'm not sorry for taking time out to accept a nice lunch from my boyfriend."

"Wait. What was that?"

Meg pulled back. "What?"

"That last part. Say it again."

She shrugged her shoulders. "What? The part about lunch?"

"No. You referred to me as your boyfriend. It's the first time you've ever given me an official title. I like the way it sounds," he said, smearing a teardrop on her cheek.

He watched as she cracked a partial smile, wanting so badly to distract her with all his love and melt her problems away.

"Well, Parker, since you brought it up, how would you justify spending just about every waking moment together for the last few months? There's something going on here, and we'd be lying if we called it a friendship."

Parker slid his fingertips down the side of her face, soaking up every inch of her soft skin. "You'll get no arguments out of me. I've been waiting for this moment. I want you and yours to be mine," he said, pecking her on the forehead. "We'll revisit this conversation because it's an important one to be had. But in the meantime, I'd love nothing more than to rescue you from that evil woman you call a boss. It seems like she's been nothing but trouble for you since the day you accepted the position at the resort."

Parker followed Meg to the living room where she laid her purse down. "Not since day one, but shortly thereafter. Hey, every job has its ups and downs. It comes along with the territory, right? I'd be in denial to think that I could get along with every single person at work the way I get along with Frankie. Speaking of Frankie, I have to get home and spend some time with her tonight. We spoke briefly, and apparently she got stuck in the elevator with some guy. Yet another piece of drama unfolding during the worst meeting in my history at The Cove."

"Ooh, is she okay?" he asked.

"Yeah, they're both fine. She was just rattled, that's all."

He slid both hands over her shoulders, gently kneading them in a way he'd hoped would be soothing to her. "I'm glad she's okay. And, as for you. I don't want you to think for one minute that you have to stay trapped in a position that makes you miserable, Meg. It's not worth it. There are plenty of other hospitality jobs on the island. Jobs working with people who will appreciate the work you do without having unrealistic expectations."

He wondered if it was wrong that he was teetering between concentrating on the issue at hand, while simultaneously enamored by her beauty. He'd come so far from when they'd first met. Finally, granting himself permission to stop hiding behind the pain of losing his late wife and unborn child. Finally, moving on and allowing himself to feel again.

Meg swung around. "Her expectations are far beyond unrealistic. She sat there in the meeting today and challenged every ounce of data that I presented. I swear she was doing it to spite me more than anything else. And, every time I would satisfy one question or justify the sales numbers, she'd slam me with something else. Even the directors were looking at her funny."

He locked eyes with her. "Whoa there. Take a deeeep breath. I know it's easier said than done, but try not to allow her to have any power or control over you. She's your boss, yes, but she still needs to respect you."

"Agreed, but that sounds so easy coming from a man who's a free agent. I, on the other hand, have to walk a fine line, knowing that if I don't, I can either take a major pay cut by finding work elsewhere, or head back to New York."

Parker gripped her gently by the arms. "You wouldn't do that to me, would you?"

"It wouldn't be intentional, but I have to be able to sustain myself out here. As it is, I've already derailed my original plan of having my own place. That's a goal I'd like to achieve sometime this century, and it's not cheap living out here on the island. At least not in the areas where I'd like to live."

"All that can be worked out. Just promise me you won't leave, Meg. Not now. Not when we've identified that we've got something real between us."

He leaned in, giving in to his urge to kiss her, no longer able to wait for a response.

Chapter 4

Frankie

With the sun setting before her and car keys in hand, Frankie paused in front of the guest telephone in the main lobby. *Should I call him? No. What for? So you can feel like a complete idiot?*

It had already been a long day and the only direction Frankie really wanted to head in was home. Besides, he was good-looking and all, but between the elevator experience and her history of making wrong decisions involving men made it seem more and more like a bad idea.

Somewhere around mid-thought, she spun around at the sound of a male's deep voice. "Hello there."

Frankie exhaled, facing Christian, who was this time wearing more casual clothing and sandals.

He glanced at the phone and then back at her. "You know, they say in order to reap the full benefits of a telephone, you have to actually pick it up and dial a number instead of staring at it. Otherwise, they serve no purpose." He chuckled.

"Ha, ha. Are you always such a wise guy? First the elevator

button jokes and now this," she said, slightly raising the corner of her mouth.

"Not really, just occasionally when I'm around a beautiful woman such as yourself."

She paused, not really knowing how to respond, except to listen as he continued.

"I was actually hoping you were considering calling me for that tour we discussed earlier. But, from the looks of things, you seem like you're ready to head home," he said, glaring down at her keys.

Suddenly feeling reinvigorated, Frankie perked up. "Yeah, that was quite the fiasco earlier today. Rumor has it that a technician was in the electrical room fooling around with the wrong set of wires. When questioned, he couldn't justify what he was doing to save his life. Needless to say, he won't be coming back to work here again. Did you receive the letter of apology this evening from the resort?" she asked.

"I did."

It felt as if his crystal blue eyes were drawing her into a soothing staring match. One that made her wonder more about who the man was beyond the good looks and charm.

She broke her gaze with a smile. "How did things turn out with your boss?"

"Um, surprisingly, he had to cancel due to an emergency of his own. So, it all worked out. Listen, I would completely understand if you just want to head home. But I'm about to grab something to eat, and I was wondering if you'd like to join me?"

Her reflection in a nearby mirror displayed the image of her face turning various shades of red. "I'm not sure that's a great idea. After today's adventure, I'm exhausted and almost certain I would make a terrible tour guide."

"Have you eaten yet?"

She stammered, tripping over the mental debate in her head.

"Well, no. But it's late and —"

Christian placed his hands together in the praying position. "Please, join me for dinner. I promise not to keep you long, and I'll even allow you to give me a raincheck for the tour."

Frankie's grin spoke volumes. "Oh really? Why, thank you for being kind enough to allow me, sir."

"I guess that sounded a little obnoxious. I'm sorry. Although, I still would like to have the personalized tour. But for now, I'm sure you can agree that it's been one heck of a day... and, well, we both need to eat. So, what do you say? Will you join me?"

Frankie could feel eyes staring, waiting for her to give a response, nearly begging her to give in. Out of her peripheral, she realized it was the evening crew at the front desk.

Clearing her throat, she said, "Just a quick bite. My roommate will be expecting me, and I'd hate to make her worry."

A dimple emerged as he responded. "Sure, there's this quaint restaurant not far from here called the Stoned Crab, if you're into seafood."

She smiled. "I know it well. I was there recently with a few girlfriends."

"Oh."

Perhaps when she exited the elevator earlier today, she may have questioned his intentions, but she didn't have to question any further. The look of disappointment that washed over his face was a telltale sign that he was interested. Even if it was only for some one-on-one conversation. The crazy thing was she'd spent so much time coaching others to get out there and meet people, yet in this moment she wasn't sure if the same advice should apply. "I'll tell you what. I don't think I'm up for a three-course meal, but if you want, we can check out Terry's Food Stand." She glanced at her watch. "She should be there for at least another hour. And she has a nice little outdoor area to sit and chat in while we grab a quick bite."

Christian nodded, then held out his hand, motioning forward. "Terry's Food Stand it is. After you, my dear."

Frankie gave him a double-take. "Are you sure? I haven't even told you what type of food she serves."

"As long as I get to spend some time getting to know you, it really doesn't matter to me," he responded.

She'd hoped her face wasn't revealing the thoughts reeling around in her head. It had to be her lucky day that a delicious-looking man would rescue her in an elevator and then take her out for a meal. Either that or somebody would have to pinch her to see if she was dreaming.

* * *

"Terry, meet Christian. He's staying at the hotel, and I thought I'd bring him by to give him a taste of Nassau, Bahamas." Frankie smiled.

The light trade winds blew Frankie's hair, exposing a beauty mark on her neck. One that Christian noticed before turning his attention to Terry. "Ms. Terry, it's so nice to meet you. I've heard nothing but great things about your menu. I can't wait to give it a try."

Terry extended her hand over the counter. "Please, just call me Terry. And, thank you for the compliment. We have plenty for you to choose from. We have johnnycakes, stew fish, crab cakes, conch salad. You name it, Darlin'."

Christian's eyes widened. "Wow, this place sounds like a full-service restaurant." He turned to Frankie and leaned in. "What's your favorite item on the menu?"

"I'm all about the crab cakes with a side of fries. Can't get enough of them. Isn't that right, Terry?"

She replied with hardy laughter. "You eat so much crab you're going to turn into one."

Terry's stand was newly established but was quickly becoming a staple for those who wanted good conversation and a taste of the Bahamas. It was the perfect spot for vacationers to stroll to and enjoy.

Christian placed the menu back on the counter. "Well, if it's that good, then how can I resist? Please, make that two crab cakes with a side of fries, please."

Terry pointed toward the area for seating. Two orders coming right up. It's rather quiet this evening. Why don't you and the lovely lady make yourselves comfortable, and I'll bring your food to you?"

Frankie winked. "Thanks, Terry. Would you mind adding a bottled water to the order?" Christian signaled to make it two.

At the table, Frankie slid across the bench while mentally searching for a topic for conversation. "So, about this tour you keep requesting. Did you have anything special in mind you wanted to see?"

He smiled. "I want to see everything. I want you to show me from your perspective why this place is ideal for couples, families, and singles alike. Why does the resort rate as high as it is?"

She folded her arms. "I'm not sure I understand what you really want to know. It's a resort with all the typical amenities that you would find anywhere else. Golf, swimming, the spa. Again, just like a designer, you get to create your own experience, whether you're single or married. You just have to be proactive and sign up for activities, that's all."

Christian raised his finger. "Oh, no. I beg to differ. I read the mission statement in The Cove's brochure. According to whoever wrote it, you're not like the other resorts, and there's something here for everyone, from the youngest to the most seasoned, and even the singles. "So—" he said, tapping his chest. "Here I am, a single guy wanting to enjoy my stay while here on business. What can I get into?"

"Okay, Christian. This is weird. I mean... I can take you around, point you in the direction of a nightclub or two, even get you a set of golf clubs so you can tee off first thing in the morning. But may I offer a suggestion before we do any of that?"

He nodded. "I'm all ears."

"Can you learn to relax first? Look around you. Take in the view. You don't see or hear anyone all uptight about being entertained based on their age or marital status. This is paradise, for goodness' sake. Enjoy it."

She watched as he nodded nonchalantly. Frankie couldn't seem to put her finger on it, but there was something about the guy that was cute, easy to talk to, yet perfect to the degree of almost being annoying. His hair was perfectly combed in place. His teeth had that bright-white Colgate smile. And then there was his obsession with the amenities of the resort. *Who is this guy?* she wondered. *And, is he interested in me or am I just imagining he is?*

Frankie released a sigh. "Okay, listen. If you're asking me for a personal tour outside of business hours, then it's an absolute must that you loosen your tie, kick back, and just enjoy yourself. If you can't agree to that, then you'll need to call the front desk and sign up for one of their tours. Technically, I probably should send you to them," she snarled.

Christian surrendered, putting up the palms of his hands. "Whoa, didn't mean to hit a sore spot."

"You didn't. It's just, if you want to experience the true magic of the Bahamas, you gotta learn to let down your hair and live a little. I realize you're here on business and all, but you know how the saying goes. All work and no play —"

"Okay, okay, I get it. No need to repeat the rest."

Terry arrived at their picnic table, placing in front of them a tray overflowing with fresh crab cakes and fries.

Frankie closed her eyes and drew in the aroma as if she were inhaling the scent for the first time. "Terry, this smells amazing."

"Why, thank you, Darlin'. I aim to deliver food that is finger licking good every time. Here's your water. Now, eat up and enjoy."

It wasn't before Christian dove into his food, leaving a small morsel resting on the corner of his mouth. "This is delicious. Good recommendation on your part."

Frankie reared back, covering her mouth, while trying to contain her laughter. "It must be good because you're wearing some of the crab on your mouth," she said, handing him a napkin.

"Thank you. My brother would get a kick out of this if he were here. He always says that I've been successful at many things in life, but learning how to eat in public wasn't one of them."

"Aww, you're fine. Just a quick dab to the left corner of your mouth and no one will ever know." She chuckled.

They continued eating, even diving into the complimentary corn on the cob that Terry had placed on the tray, before Frankie broke the silence. "So, what are some of your successes and accomplishments?"

Christian looked up. "Excuse me?"

"Your brother... he said you've been successful at many things. Name one."

Again, he gave her the most perfect and sweet smile, exposing his dimples. "Oh, nothing crazy. I once earned a car salesman of the year award. I used to sell cars right after college. That was back when I was still trying to figure out what I wanted to do with my life."

"Really? That's neat. I may have asked you earlier, but what do you do for a living?"

He paused, seemingly thinking about a way to answer. "Well, it's kind of complicated, but in a nutshell —"

She noticed him looking around. "Are you a secret service agent, staying here at the resort on a mission?" She giggled.

"Kind of. I am an investigator, if you will. And what I do for a living pretty much falls under the top-secret category. If I tell anyone, I could lose my job."

Frankie paused, not knowing how to read him. Her flesh wanted to press further, questioning his line of work. The other part of her brain thought the element of secrecy was sexy. "Stop! Are you serious? My uncle used to go on top-secret missions while serving in the military. He could only share unclassified information, but I used to always think his job was so mysterious and exciting."

Christian grunted. "Oh, it's exciting all right. But enough about me. I want to know more about you."

Trying her best not to grin, she continued. "Well, I already told you about my gig. What else is there to know?"

He put his fork down, giving her his undivided attention. "Surely there's more to you than your title in HR. When I look across the table, I see a beautiful woman who clearly has a sense of adventure that lies within. If not, you wouldn't have given me such a hard time about enjoying the magic of the Bahamas," he blurted, followed by a huge smile.

"Good observation on your part. What else do you see when you look into my eyes?" she asked, finding herself flirting just a bit.

Christian stared for a moment. "I see curiosity. But I also

saw fear in the elevator earlier today. Perhaps because of something traumatic from your past?"

It felt like everything on the inside of her dropped into a bottomless pit, instantly bringing her appetite to a halt.

"Yeah, about that. Sorry you had to witness me freaking out. It was a rare moment that very few ever witness," she said, looking downward.

Christian slid his hand across the table. "Hey, there's no need to apologize. Maybe I shouldn't have brought it up. But you just seemed so upset earlier. I'm not a professional — but maybe I can be an ear."

Everything that was pleasant about the evening came to an abrupt halt for Frankie, like a car slamming on its brakes. "It's a personal matter. And, while I thank you for the offer, it's getting rather late. I probably should head home," she said, feverishly scrambling to close her food containers, drawing the conversation to an end.

Chapter 5

Meg

Back at the house, Meg showered and slipped into comfortable clothing. Tomorrow would be a work from home day, her absolute favorite days. The flexibility allowed her to bypass the routine of preparing lunch and selecting an outfit, but unfortunately, it gave her more time to stew over her day with Iris.

A hard knock on the door snatched her out of the mental reenactment of the day's events. "Come in," she called.

Her roomie peered inside.

"Frankie, there you are. It's not like you to come in this late," Meg said.

Frankie leaned against the door. "You're not the only one with a life outside of work, you know. Every once in a while, I like to go out and have some fun," she replied, twirling a lock of hair.

Meg's eyebrows folded. "If I find out that you went on one of your island adventures without me I'm going to be upset, Frankie Jones."

Frankie playfully rolled her eyes. "You know, it's pretty

pathetic when people always assume that I'm either on a solo adventure or sitting home alone. Never once did it cross your mind that I might be on a date?"

"Not really," Meg blurted, then covered her mouth. "I didn't mean it the way it sounded. It's just, if you were going on a date, wouldn't you have mentioned it to me when we spoke earlier? You talked about the elevator incident, which sounded awful, by the way, but you never said a word about a date."

A lazy smile washed over Frankie's face as she fully entered the room, making herself comfortable. "Okay, fine. You're right. I wasn't on a date, but I did grab dinner with a guy tonight."

"Oooh. Who's the lucky guy?"

For as long as Meg had known Frankie, she hadn't invested a lot of time in dating. She mentioned something a while back about an online situation that led her to move to the Bahamas. And, when that didn't work out, she kept her chin up instead of losing hope, believing that her guy was out there somewhere. But, again, none of that really added up to actually getting out there and dating.

Frankie fumbled as she tried to explain. "Well, he's — This is going to sound so ridiculous."

Meg's eyelids widened. "Elevator man! It's elevator man, isn't it?"

Both women burst into an ongoing spell of laughter for several minutes.

Frankie continued. "Yeah, I guess that would be an appropriate nickname for him. Elevator man, a.k.a. Christian," she said, still easing out of the laughter. "We ran into each other down in the lobby, and since neither of us had eaten, we decided to grab a bite from Terry's."

Meg rubbed her hands together. "This is awesome. I needed a good pick-me-up story after this afternoon. Tell me everything that happened from start to finish."

"I hate to burst your bubble, but there's not much to tell. Actually, there is one small tidbit of information. The guy has been begging me to give him a tour of the resort. That's all he could seem to talk about in the elevator and again this evening. He has some sort of obsession with learning everything we offer for singles and knowing everything about the resort in general. I'd almost consider his level of curiosity to be a little strange if it weren't because he really seems to have a busy work schedule. He probably just needs an outlet to get out and have fun like the rest of us. Who knows?"

Meg placed her finger over her lip. "Hmm, and of all the agencies he could book a tour with, he asked you to be his personal guide? You must've had a pretty good conversation in the elevator together. I like this guy. Tell me more."

"Again, I hate to burst your bubble, but there wasn't much to it. I introduced myself. I ended up telling him what I do for the resort because he helped me with my big rolling cart stacked with HR papers, and then —"

Meg watched Frankie as she scanned her eyes across the room. "And then what? You're killing me here, Frankie. I want to know how you got from HR papers on a rolling cart to dinner!"

"Okay, fine. We kissed in the elevator and it was so steamy and passionate I nearly lost my mind," Frankie said.

Meg's mouth dropped. "What? Get... out... of... freaking... town! There's no way!"

Frankie laughed. "You're right. I'm lying. But it was still fun watching your facial expression as I said it."

Meg looked for the nearest pillow, chucking it across the room. "You're so rotten, Frankie. Will you tell me what really happened already?"

"Hey, a girl's gotta have a little fun. But, seriously speaking, this is ridiculous. We're making too much of it. Really! We talked for a little in the elevator to keep our minds occupied, and who knows. I may or may not have imagined a little flirting, or extra glances exchanged. But, I promise you, that's all there is to it."

Meg, being the detailed woman that she was, folded her arms, signaling Frankie to continue.

"And — when I finally got off the elevator, he may have asked me to call him sometime. But, that was just to arrange a tour. That's all. I even decided against calling him when I was passing through the lobby tonight, but as fate would have it, we bumped into each other and the rest is history," Frankie said, sweeping her hands together.

The phone rang, causing Meg to grunt. "Hold that thought. You're not getting off the hook that easily."

On the other end of the line, a brief exchange with Parker confirmed the details of his upcoming party. Something they would've discussed further if their visit hadn't ended with more kissing and less conversation.

Meg hung up the phone. "Sorry about that. Before I forget, I hope your calendar is wide open for Saturday. Parker is throwing a last-minute pool party at the beach house. He wants to celebrate the end of another great project and he said it will be a fun way to close out the summer."

Frankie nodded. "Saturday at the beach house. Got it. I'll be there. Is he sure about throwing a party at a place he just renovated?"

"We'll all be outdoors. I'm sure it will be fine. By the way, I think this would be the perfect opportunity for you to take your elevator friend on a little detour. Show off the resort, then bring him with you to the party on Saturday. We're all gathering around three. I'll text you the address," Meg said.

"Are you nuts? I'm not asking him to come to my friend's

party. I barely know the guy. It will send all the wrong signals, making him think that I'm into him," Frankie said.

A slow smile unveiled as Meg rose out of her chair. "From your expression when you talk about him, I think the idea is definitely worth exploring."

* * *

After completing the last task for the week, Meg put on her tennis shoes, making a bee-line for the center of town. She desperately needed an outlet and had been eyeing an invitation posted in the front window of Sabrina's bookstore. It was a quaint antique-ish looking place, with a sign inviting women to join their weekly book club. Word around the island was that the club was a place where women could let their hair down, spill the tea, but also a wonderful place where friendships were formed. *What do I have to lose?* Meg thought. So, she decided to give it a try.

The aroma of freshly brewed hazelnut coffee nearly consumed all of her senses. She pressed inward, hearing the sound of a bell ringing overhead.

A lady in a bright sundress came over. "Good afternoon, welcome to Sabrina's Bookstore. I'm Sabrina, and you are?" she asked, showing her pearly white teeth while extending her hand.

"Meg."

"Nice to meet you, Meg. Is your name short for —"

"Megan. But, I usually stick with Meg."

Sabrina nodded. "Meg, it's a pleasure having you. Is this your first time visiting the store?"

"It is, but I understand you host a weekly book club and I thought I'd come check it out." Meg turned, referencing the front window. "The sign in the window, advertising the book of the month. I was wondering if I'm not too late for—" She hesitated.

"The group started about a half-hour ago, but I'm sure they don't mind you joining in. Do you need a copy of the book?"

Meg glanced around, noticing a little bantering back and forth as they gathered toward the back of the store. Of all the things to do on a late Friday afternoon, including working out on the beach, she still wasn't sure if this was a good idea.

She noticed Sabrina motioning toward the front table. "I still have several copies left. And, I promise you haven't missed much. This is only week two, and from what I can tell, the discussion is starting to heat up." She leaned in closer. "Trust me, this is where the ladies come to have a good time. Why don't you take a copy and spend the next hour with the girls? If you like the group, you can purchase the book. If not, you can leave it behind on the table. No one will have to know."

Meg began following Sabrina. "You really don't have to do that," she whispered.

Sabrina winked and pointed her in the direction of the last empty chair in the back. Feeling like a shy young girl on the first day of school, she looked around, trying to figure out what chapter everyone was discussing.

One of the members chimed in. "I, for one, think the main character has a lot of deeply rooted issues she needs to deal with. There's no way she can have a successful relationship in the future if she doesn't address her skeletons first. Starting with that lying, cheating, son of a sea biscuit, husband of hers. Can you believe she's still allowing him to live in the basement after everything he put her through? If I found my husband in the middle of a rendezvous with another woman, I'd kick him out so fast he might catch a bad case of whiplash!" she said, causing an outburst of laughter among the women.

Another member chimed in. "Yes, but I think we need to

challenge ourselves to look beyond the surface here. There's usually a reason behind every decision we make. This woman lost her mother, has an aunt with stage four cancer, and the icing on the cake — the man she planned on spending the rest of her life with had an affair, not once, but twice. Do you think it's possible she's at the end of her rope? Maybe worn out from the pain associated with loss and even willing to sacrifice her happiness, just to hold on to something familiar?"

You could barely hear a pin drop in the room.

A recognizable feeling bubbled over on the inside of Meg. It was the same feeling she had when her mind started racing with passionate opinions mixed with real-life experiences to reference. She slowly raised a finger. "Hi, I'm new here and — I'm not sure what you discussed last week, but I'd have to agree with the last comment. Sometimes when you're exhausted with your circumstances, but not quite ready to let go, you find yourself compromising and doing the very thing you never thought you would do," she said, skimming over the words on the page. "Perhaps this character, Shelby, is it? Perhaps she hasn't quite reached her breaking point. Maybe that's the reason why she's allowing him to remain in the house."

The first member who spoke up chimed in again. "Well, how much breaking does one need to realize her husband has an issue with monogamy? And, what does that have to do with her mother's death or her aunt's illness? Wouldn't you think she'd rather have a man that's supportive by her side?"

Meg cleared her throat, mentally trying to coach herself into holding her tongue but knowing ultimately she wouldn't listen to her inner voice. "Ma'am, I for one lost my mother many years ago, when I was a teenager. Those were some of the most precious years of my life when I needed her most. Sure, I learned to deal with it, but behind the scenes I was a mess, imagining what it would be like to go to prom without her there to help me pick out a dress or to prepare for my wedding day without her by my side."

Sitting on the edge of her seat, Meg wiped her forehead, removing beads of sweat that were starting to form. "I even went as far as allowing people into my life that didn't belong, just so I didn't have to feel lonely. And, I did this even though I had the support of my father growing up. How many women have you met that endured a three-year engagement, knowing they should've broken it off after year one?" She paused, then continued in a stern tone. "He was a cheating son-of-a-gun, just like Shelby's man. Why did I do it? Why did I stay with him for so long? Who knows? Probably because I was trying to fill a void. An empty void that a lying man could never fill. No one could heal the wounds that caused me to make such poor decisions back then... and no one can heal those wounds now." She paused again, then said, "It's easy to judge these characters, like she said, but it's a completely different thing to actually walk a mile in their shoes."

Immediately Meg retreated, resting her back on the chair. Her bubbling passion had fizzled, leaving her with a sense that she'd shocked the heck out of every woman in the group. She'd even shocked herself by speaking so candidly.

One by one, the women began clapping. The original woman who criticized Shelby's character began to speak. "I stand corrected," she said, holding her book in the air. "Ladies, we need to start having more real conversations, like the one we're having tonight. And, if a book like this can be the impetus for these kinds of discussions, then I'm all for it. Now, I don't mean to put you on the spot, and you certainly don't have to answer. But if you're willing, I'd like to know what kind of advice you'd give to a character like Shelby. How does one see their way out of a continuous spiral of wrong decision-making, just to fill an empty void?"

Meg tapped her finger on the pages of her book, realizing she was no more qualified to answer that question than she had been when she was a teenager. She was still leaping from one decision to another, running away from all that was bad, while perhaps discovering the one thing that was good, which was Parker.

"That's a million-dollar question," Meg said, closing her book. "A question I'm still trying to work my way through. Perhaps the answer will be revealed to us all by the time we get to the end of this book."

Chapter 6

Parker

Parker dialed the last three digits of old man Barnes' telephone number. He figured it would be a courtesy call at best. Then he'd return to odds and ends around the house and perhaps run a few errands for the party. No big deal. Around the fifth ring someone picked up, filling the line with silence. If it weren't for the sound of a microwave chiming in the background, he'd almost question if the line was still open.

"Hello?" Parker said.

"Who's calling?" the man's voice barked.

"My name is Parker Wilson. A friend of mine gave me your number. He said you wanted to —"

The rattling sound of the man's cough dominated the telephone, interrupting his introduction. When the old man was finished, he bellowed out a few words.

"Well, you certainly took long enough to reach out. Is this the way you normally do business?"

"Sir?"

Again, the man bellowed, "I'm not sure what Chuck told

you, but I'm a businessman. Which means that I like to do things in an orderly fashion and I don't like wasting time."

Parker paused in front of the refrigerator. "Well, that would make two of us, sir. I told Chuck I'd give you a courtesy call, but I—"

"Look, I'm going to cut to the chase," he said, while again battling a rattling cough that darn near sounded like he could cough up a lung.

When he got himself together, he continued. "I've been conducting some research on you and your company. As a result, I'd like to meet to discuss a proposition. I don't conduct meetings over the phone. Never have and I never will. If you're interested in hearing more, meet me at 3009 Seaside Drive in an hour."

Parker rubbed his temple. "An hour? Sir, with all due respect, I don't really know much about you outside of a word or two from the locals, but —"

"Ah, what do they know?" he barked. "Outside of nick-naming me Old Man Barnes, they don't have a clue about who I am. Leave it up to people to stay at your bed-and-breakfast a few times and then claim to know it all."

"Okay." Parker didn't know whether to apologetically bow out of the chance to meet or what. Something told him if he tried, he'd personally feel the wrath of old man Barnes, just as he'd experienced so far. "You know what? It's not a problem. Seaside Drive is on the way to where I'm going this evening, so I'd be happy to stop by in about an hour."

"Good," Mr. Barnes replied. "And don't be late. Time is money." With that being said, the old man hung up the phone.

Parker questioned why he was on the receiving end of people hanging up on him this week, but one thing for certain, Chuck already owed him big time, and it would probably be even worse by the time the meeting with old man Barnes concluded.

* * *

Parker slammed the door to his pickup while surveying the area. It was just as Chuck had described, except even better. Two beach houses used as a bed-and-breakfast with cottage-like charm. Both were set back from the street with extensive views of the water on one side and touristy shops on the other. The homes appeared large enough to house multiple families and in between the two properties was a gift shop. All three were a little run down in appearance, but nothing a little paint couldn't fix.

Here goes nothing, he thought, as he climbed a few steps leading to house number 3009. A wooden sign hung above the door that read Seaside B&B.

Before Parker could knock, the door creaked ajar, leaving a small glimpse of a man hunched slightly while walking away. The familiar cough from the telephone line echoed from the hall as the man yelled for him to come in.

"Mr. Barnes?" Parker said, slowly pushing the door further ajar.

"The one and only. Come in and close the door behind you."

Inside, Parker was greeted by old floral wallpaper that probably easily dated back to the late eighties, maybe even earlier. But the crown molding, and original hardwoods, and even the beautiful guest parlor were enough to take one's breath away. At least it captivated his attention until he looked up to see old man Barnes staring at him.

"Sorry, I couldn't help but stop and take it all in. I haven't seen a place like this since I arrived here. And, that's coming from someone who's renovated quite a few homes."

The old man waved a mahogany cane towards the couch, signaling for him to sit down.

"I know a lot about you, and that's the reason I asked you to join me this evening. You have the kind of experience under your belt that I'm looking for."

Parker waved. "Mr. Barnes, I'm not sure what you're looking for, but this kind of job isn't exactly in line with what I do," he said, hesitating to continue. He observed as the man sat, watching him with a stern expression on his face.

Mr. Barnes pulled out a handkerchief and proceeded to speak. "That's the problem with young folks today. They do a whole lot of talking and very little listening."

A moment of silence followed before Parker continued. "Okay then. In an effort not to waste your time, I'm curious to know... why did you invite me here today?"

"I received word about a very skilled man who works on homes here in Nassau, helping them return to their original beauty."

Parker excitedly chimed in, "Yes, that's me. I like to —" Immediately picking up on Barnes' stiff disposition, Parker's words trailed off to silence. "Sorry, sir. What were you saying again?"

"As I was saying, I've heard a lot about you. A skilled man from Chicago who can renovate the heck out of a home from top to bottom, creating turnkey designs that are highly sought after by many. So, I started conducting a little research, trying to learn more about this man they call Parker Wilson, figuring maybe one day his services may be of use to me here at the B&B."

This time Parker didn't say a word, but instead suppressed the urge to shift in his seat as he tried to figure out what he would say next. Maybe the key reason Old Man Barnes called him over was to help him with a quick fixer upper job, so he could turn around and make a quick sale. Although, anyone willing to buy the place could tell that it needed reviving.

Mr. Barnes continued. "Then after I got to digging around and asking questions, I found out you have quite the story," he said with a partial smile. It was the first time the corner of his lip curled upward since Parker arrived.

Barnes cleared his throat. "Turns out there's more to your background than simply chasing run-down houses."

Parker swallowed loud enough that he wondered if Barnes could hear him. "Sir? I'm not sure that I follow," he replied.

The old man grunted. "Sure you do. You have history with a woman by the name of Jenna Maxwell, don't you?"

"Yes, although I'm not sure what Jenna would have to do with my visit here today. I got the impression from Chuck that you were looking for someone to help you with the property."

Barnes continued, practically ignoring Parker. "Evelyn always wondered what happened to the poor girl. She'd become fond of having her around as a volunteer. We had no idea Jenna was terminally ill."

Parker imagined himself immediately calling Chuck once he returned to the truck. If this was his idea of doing him a favor, then he definitely needed to go back to the drawing board.

He stood up. "I'm sorry. I'm not really sure how you knew Jenna, but —"

Old Man Barnes barked. "Make yourself comfortable. I'm not finished yet. I have no intention of ruffling your feathers this evening, if that's what you're thinking. I think by the time you leave here, you'll find the visit was well worth the effort. Now, what was I saying?"

Parker eased back onto the couch. "You were talking about Jenna," he mumbled.

"Yes, Jenna Maxwell. A nice young lady indeed. At least, according to Evelyn, she was. I didn't know her very well, but my late wife Evelyn did. Their group spent time volunteering together at the homeless shelter. Evelyn had a knack for giving back and apparently Jenna did as well."

Parker relaxed at the mere mention of the homeless shelter. Mr. Barnes was right. It was Jenna's passion to give back. She recognized that even in places like the beautiful Nassau Bahamas, there were people in need, and she always felt like it was her duty to serve.

He chuckled. "That was Jenna, alright. I'm sorry, but I don't recall her ever mentioning Mrs. Barnes by name."

"My wife probably went by the name Eve. That's what everyone called her for short. She used to come home with endless stories about recipes the group shared as they prepared meals to be served. No one would've ever known that Evelyn was the owner of a beachside B&B. She would've easily kept it to herself, always being humble and always looking for opportunities to do something for someone else, even if it meant stretching herself beyond her limits. She didn't care. At the shelter, she grew fond of Jenna over their shared love of soup... split pea, chicken soup, bean soup... the list was endless, if I can recall correctly."

Parker nodded. "Yessir, that was definitely Jenna Maxwell, for sure. She was the only woman I knew who carried on and on about hot soup recipes in the middle of the hot summer here in the Bahamas. Of all the things to eat!"

Mr. Barnes cracked a smile. "I can relate. Evelyn was the head chef here at the B&B. She always got a kick out of playing every role except the most important one of all. She used to say, no one will care about my title as owner, but they'll have a whole lot to say about the B&B if they think the food tastes bad." His smile lingered a while longer, then soon faded as he gazed away from Parker.

"Mr. Barnes, until now I had completely forgotten about Jenna's time spent at the shelter. Our last couple of months together were focused solely on her deteriorating health. She could've mentioned your wife, but if she did, I don't recall."

Mr. Barnes replied, "It's fine. I didn't bring you here to dig up old wounds. I know what it's like to lose someone who means the world to you. In that sense, we're one in the same. If you look around this place, it's evident my world has been crumbling to pieces ever since my Evelyn left me. It's part of the reason why I asked Chuck to reach out to you on my behalf."

"What can I do for you?" Parker asked.

A long period of silence echoed throughout the parlor-like setting as Mr. Barnes gathered his thoughts.

"Wilson, I'll admit that I'm struggling, trying desperately to set my pride aside so I can properly bring closure to this business. But this isn't easy. This B&B is the last connection I have to my late wife, Evelyn. I can close my eyes and envision her cooking for the guests, preparing the living quarters, and even getting after me for not interacting with everyone. I'm not much of a people person if you couldn't tell."

Parker nearly had spit flying as he mistakenly let a chuckle slip, then he quickly regained control of himself. "I'm sorry. Please continue."

"It took every part of my being to pick up the phone and dial Chuck Nesbit. We tossed around a few ideas about how I could sell in a way I can feel good about it, instead of having to suffer a loss or foreclosure of some sort. The bank is after me for what I owe, but there's still a small window of time to redeem myself, and that's where you, Evelyn, and Jenna come in."

Parker's eyes widened. "I'm sorry? I'm not sure that I follow. Jenna and Mrs. Barnes are no longer here and as for me..." he stuttered. "I don't see where I fit in."

Old man Barnes scooted to the edge of his seat, leaning in closely. "I believe Evelyn put it on my heart to offer this business to you."

"What?" Parker reared back.

"Hear me out. At first, I had it in mind to ask you to help me spruce the place up. I figured a quick paint job, maybe some new carpet, and fresh new furniture for the terrace would do. Then, I'd put out the for sale sign and try to salvage as much of a profit as I could before the bank came knocking on the door looking for their share. That's when it hit me like a ton of bricks!"

"Sir —"

"Now, hold on, Wilson. I need you to listen to everything I have to say. Then you can give me your honest feedback."

Parker allowed a silent sigh to ease out, slumping back even further into the couch. When Mr. Barnes stared at him, he waved, giving him the signal to go on.

"Wilson, think long and hard about what I'm about to say. You're already in the business of renovating homes, correct?" Barnes asked.

"Yes, renovating and then selling. A bit different from running a whole B&B, wouldn't you say?"

Barnes nodded. "Yes, yes, there are some differences, but nothing you can't handle. Heck, even I've been doing this for two years now, and people don't even like me the way they loved Evelyn. I don't have the personality and charm it takes to pull this off indefinitely. Plus, I'm suffering from a broken heart — too many difficult memories. But, you! I can't think of a better person to make this place shine again, while living on site. Getting this place up to par again is half the battle. The rest practically runs itself because of the location. To make things even better, you'd have a ready-made staff... well, almost ready-made. You'd probably need a new manager who can take care of hospitality. Maybe even another clerk for the gift shop, but you could make it work. In the end, all you'd have to do is sit back and be the overseer of the actual business while you renovate. And, I promise, within a year's time, if this business isn't turning the kind of profit you'd hoped for, then sell it for triple or even quadruple what you paid. It's that simple."

"No! Sorry, no can do." Parker bounced up. "We're talking well beyond the scope of my expertise. I know nothing about running a B&B. Absolutely nothing."

"Neither did I, but Evelyn taught me everything I needed to know, and I can teach you. Look, there are two things that stood out to me when I called Nesbit. One... you have what it takes to turn this place around, whether it be for a long-term business that you run hands on, or a business you oversee from afar. And, if those options don't work for you, it can even be a business that you just renovate and turn for a profit if you see fit. Although, I'd like to think you'd give the other options a try first."

"Mr. Barnes, this is crazy."

"Don't you want to hear the second thing that stood out to me?"

Parker ran his fingers through his hair, feeling almost numb. "I'll bet you're going to tell me."

"It's something Evelyn used to talk about after volunteering with Jenna."

Parker slowly looked up. "Let me guess, Jenna used to secretly dream about owning a B&B without ever telling me about it?"

"No. She talked about how much she adored you. And how much of a good man you are. Heck, Evelyn used to come home and talk about you all so much. It even made me a little jealous." He smiled, then continued. "Then at some point the conversations faded when Evelyn lost touch with Jenna. She missed her for quite a while. And wondered why she'd stopped coming to the homeless center." His voice faded. "Anyway, I figured if you were the highlight of their conversation over hot soup, and the most popular name around the island — well, then you must be a pretty decent man."

Old man Barnes got up and shuffled over to the credenza, where he began pouring water into his glass. "And, it goes without saying, Wilson... not only are you a savvy businessman, but in some ways we're a lot alike. I don't know of one other person on this island living in a property that exists as their primary business. To be honest, it's not even the Bahamian way unless you're in the hotel industry. The folks out here are laid back, spending all their leisure time soaking up the sun when they're not at work. Not constantly living and breathing their next business strategy like us."

Parker interrupted, "While I agree that entrepreneurs have that extra drive, Mr. Barnes, I can almost hear the locals now. Parker Wilson... the new owner of Seaside B&B? It doesn't make any sense."

"Give it time, Wilson. Chew on it. Let it marinate for a little while."

Parker watched Mr. Barnes as he scratched something down on paper. "I need to excuse myself. The old kidneys don't work the way they used to. While I'm gone, I'd like for you to wander around and take a tour of the B&B. Make yourself feel at home. While you're doing so, mull over these numbers and perhaps give me a call by the end of the week. I can almost guarantee with the kind of effort you're putting into moving around from place to place, you can comfortably reap a healthy salary right here, while still having plenty of time to live the island life." He passed the paper along. "If you're concerned about having enough renovation work to do, you'd have over approximately ten thousand square feet between the two houses plus the store. I think that should keep you busy for a while," he said, exiting the room.

Parker held the paper up. "Mr. Barnes, I feel bad that you're in this predicament, but I'm almost certain I'm not the right guy for the deal."

Old Man Barnes called over his shoulder, "I'm almost certain you're wrong. Tour the house, Wilson, and read over the numbers. Then come back during the week for another visit during the day. Time is not on my side, so I'll need to hear back from you by the end of the week," he said, then continued down the long hall, stopping to say one last thing. "By the way, we have a guest staying upstairs in the Coral room, so it goes without saying you'll have to see that room at a later time."

Parker stood by himself, staring at double glass doors that appeared to be the entrance of a dining room. *This guy has lost his mind,* he thought. He tucked the paper in his pocket and figured, as a courtesy, he'd complete the self-guided tour before making a bee-line for the front door.

Chapter 7

Frankie

"Hi, may I have room one-twelve please?" Frankie asked, while wedging the phone between her ear and shoulder. It was just past the nine o'clock hour the last time she glanced, giving her plenty of time to fiddle around on a Saturday morning. Also plenty of time to catch Christian and apologize for her abrupt departure.

"Frankie?" he answered.

"How did you know it was me?"

"I don't know anyone else who would dial my room on a Saturday morning," he said.

"Not even your boss?" she asked, once again allowing curiosity to get the best of her.

"Not even my boss, thankfully. We normally follow a typical work week."

She smiled to herself. "Well, that rules out the military and potentially the secret service. Those guys are practically on call twenty-four-seven."

Christian snickered on the other end of the line. "Still trying to figure out my occupation, I see."

"Pretty much, but I'll leave it alone for now, Mr. Top Secret. I really called to apologize for taking off the way I did yesterday. You were kind enough to treat me to Terry's, and the least I could've done was stuck around to finish the meal."

"Hey, I touched on a sore spot, I get it. I'm the one who should be apologizing. I'm actually glad you called. It wasn't until you left last night that I realized I have no way of contacting you, except for random encounters in the front lobby if I'm lucky. If I had your number, I would've definitely called to apologize."

Frankie eased into the rocking chair on her front porch with a partial smile slowly emerging. "Well, how about we start fresh and give ourselves a clean slate? My name is Frankie Jones. What's yours?"

"She likes to roleplay, I see. Um, okay. Hold on, let me get into character."

Frankie giggled. "Just be yourself, silly."

"I know. I got this. Okay, here goes. My name is Christian Halstead. The guy you met the other day at the resort."

"Hmm, Christian Halstead. I like that name. It has a nice ring to it."

"Why, thank you. I uh... I called you this morning because I have something pretty important to ask you."

Again, Frankie giggled, but this time with butterflies fluttering on the inside. "I called you, remember?"

Christian returned to his normal voice. "Okay, Ms. Jones, if we're going to do this right, you have to overlook the minor details and flow with me."

She cleared her throat. "Yes, of course. Where were we?"

"We were at the part where I was about to ask you on a date. A breakfast date here at the resort — sort of like a do-over for last night."

Silence consumed the line as Frankie's pulse started to race. It was such a sweet moment. Yet she genuinely didn't know what to say. The last time a guy seriously asked her out was so long ago, leading to a long-distance fiasco that ended in a break-up. *Frankie, it's just breakfast. Calm down,* she told herself.

"Sure, except how about we put a twist on breakfast?"

"What did you have in mind?" he asked.

"Well, it's such a beautiful morning. Why don't we grab something to go and take a walk along the beach? Maybe even pass by the resort, so I can give you that tour you've been asking about."

"I love the idea of taking a morning stroll with you, but I don't want this to turn into work. I want to get to know you — no strings attached."

"And I'd like to get to know you. Trust me. There will be no work involved. Just two people getting together to enjoy each other's company. Deal?"

"You've got yourself a deal. Can I pick you up?" he asked.

"Um, how about we meet downstairs in the lobby at The Cove, grab something to go from one of the eateries downstairs, and head out to the beach from there?"

"Can you be there in an hour?" he asked.

"I'll see you then."

Frankie hung up, holding the phone in her hand for a solid minute, trying to process what happened. As not to get her hopes up, she chalked it up to *just breakfast.* Then she'd spend the afternoon at her friend's pool party, and life would continue on as usual. No big deal.

* * *

"You definitely get an A plus for spontaneity, Halstead." Frankie smiled, catching herself staring as he bit into his breakfast sandwich. If this guy's looks could kill, she'd be in trouble.

He nodded. "Turns out I'm not the only spontaneous one. I was shocked you called me this morning. For a minute there, I thought we might not see each other again."

Stunned at the comment, she said, "With the number of times I have to schlep that cart back and forth to the conference room, I doubt it. We were bound to see each other again, unless you're checking out this evening. How long is your stay again?"

"I'm here until the end of the week. Then I'm being rerouted to a new location for my next assignment. I guess you could say my schedule is somewhat all over the map these days."

The corner of her mouth raised into a lazy smile as she casually noticed a tattoo on the inner portion of his wrist. The tattoo had the initials A.H.

Christian also looked down, then held his wrist outward. "Anna Halstead. She's my sister. She died in a car crash early last year."

A feeling of guilt for bringing attention to it washed over Frankie. "I just happened to notice as you waved your arm. I'm so sorry for your loss."

"Thanks. Seems kind of silly that a forty-seven-year-old would walk around with his sister's initials on his wrist, but she was my best friend. And, now that she's gone — I don't know, I guess it's my small way of holding on to her memory. A tribute, if you will."

They continued walking while finishing the remaining remnants of breakfast on the beach.

"Where's home base when you're not traveling?" she asked.

"That's a good question. My home office is in Atlanta, Georgia, but I don't stay there long enough to call it home. I always find myself traveling, like somewhat of a nomad, if you will."

He stopped long enough to look Frankie in the eyes, triggering goosebumps to raise on her forearms. To combat the awkwardness, she threw a new topic at him. "Well, since we managed to devour these sandwiches, are you ready for that tour? If you want to see things from behind the scenes, then you're definitely hanging with the right girl."

"Um, sure. But at some point along the way, I'll have to interrupt this tour for a surprise," he said.

Frankie tilted her head. "Hmm, he's spontaneous and filled with surprises. I like it."

"This is our first date, and I'm determined to make a good first impression. Don't think for one minute I haven't noticed your subtle way of trying to hijack the date. The man is supposed to lead, planning something special for the woman."

She stopped in her tracks. "Excuse me, sir. But you've been asking me for the tour from the moment we stepped foot in the elevator. And while I'm thankful chivalry isn't dead, I see nothing wrong with a little input from both parties."

"Touché, touché," he responded, raising his hands in the air.

As they approached one of the most beautiful stretches of the beach filled with miniature beach cabins for miles, she stopped to show it off. It was a newly created spot she most often wished she had a companion to walk hand-in-hand with. The latest addition to the resort, where lovers and singles alike hung out.

Frankie closed her eyes. "I could literally stay out here all day, allowing the sound of the waves to wash my cares away. I'd take a little dip in the water, and then come back and relax in a hut, maybe read a magazine or just take in the sun. Plus, I absolutely adore the five-star set up with the umbrellas and cabins, don't you?" She giggled.

"Ahh, she appreciates the finer things, and she's classy. I like it. How about we claim this hut over here?" he said, placing his items down, then swiftly removing his shirt, watch, and sandals. "You said you like spontaneity, right?" Christian asked.

"Sure but, what about our walk along the beach, and the tour of the resort and —"

She hesitated, but all Christian could seem to do was shed his articles of clothing down to his swimming trunks.

"Well, I was thinking, since we both like the water and we both like spontaneity, perhaps we'd go for a quick swim then come back for a little more conversation."

She glanced down at her clothing. Sure, she'd put on a bathing suit underneath her shorts and linen tunic, but it was more so for the look than anything else. She didn't expect to be fully submerged in the water with this bare-chested hunk of a man, not the same guy she'd only met earlier in the week.

Christian teased. "Sooo, you're either afraid to go in the water or I'm making you terribly uncomfortable right now — in which case, I'll put my shirt back on because that's not my intention."

Frankie raised her finger, putting an end to the ridiculous notion. "Me? Afraid to go in the water? You don't know who you're dealing with. They don't call me adventurous for nothing."

But before she could finish her sentence, Christian took off, running toward the ocean so fast she could hardly keep up.

* * *

With wet curls dangling behind her neckline, Frankie slowed down and began showcasing the grounds. "First stop, an eighteen-hole golf course where luxury meets the Bahamian Breeze. A perfect retreat for golfers, especially single golfers, if you will. I know that opportunities for singles seem to be a priority for you," Frankie teased.

"Look, in my defense, I think it's important that if resorts like The Cove are going to command such a high price tag per night, then they should be prepared to accommodate everyone's needs," he said, then pointed toward the course. "Wow, pretty impressive course for those who like the game."

Frankie laughed. "Ooh, do I hear a little optimism in your voice?"

"What you hear is me being open-minded," he said, then he removed one of her wet curls that managed to get tangled in her earring. "By the way, the whole curly, wet hairdo looks attractive on you."

An electric current ran through her veins as he grazed her neck, leaving her feeling so exhilarated. But she knew all too well the dangers of falling for the small gestures. So she pressed on, vowing not to give it too much attention.

"Thank you. Now, Mr. Open Minded, perhaps you'd enjoy a stroll through the casino," she said, taking a turn toward a path leading back to the main building of the resort.

Christian chuckled while trying to catch up. "I play a mean game of war, but outside of that, I'm not much of a gambler. There's something about putting your money on the table, knowing it could disappear in a matter of minutes —" he said, snapping his finger. "It just makes me nervous. My grandpa always emphasized the importance of saving, instilling a healthy fear in me, I suppose."

Frankie dug her hands into the pockets of her jean shorts while contemplating everything he saying. "There's nothing wrong with living according to your family values. I strongly believe that not everything is for everybody, and if it isn't for you, you shouldn't indulge."

A warm smile appeared on Christian's face. "Name one family value that you still live by today."

"Ohh, I have quite a few up my sleeve. But, hmm, let's see. Growing up in my household, you would always hear mom say, keep God first in all that you do, always be true to yourself, and always be loyal to your family and friends. I'd like to think I still live by all the above, but I'm not so sure my parents would agree."

"What makes you say that?" he asked.

She looked into his eyes, realizing he'd listen to her entire life story if she felt like telling it. He was easy to talk to. Even more easy to stroll side-by-side with and she liked it.

"My parents didn't exactly approve of the way I packed up my life and left to come here," she explained.

"I'm sure you were chasing your dreams or in search of starting a new life here on the island. Not exactly something to be upset about. Plenty of people do it," Christian responded.

"Ha, you make things sound so simple, but that's not quite how it went. I came here from the UK, searching for love. Or at least what I thought was love at the time. He turned out to be everything but love, which, of course, gave my family enough fuel to say I told you so. But, when I decided to plant roots here and settle in, making this my new home, that's when the distance began to grow between us."

Christian eased his hand over her shoulder. "Yikes, I'm sorry. If this is another sore spot, just say the word and we can move on to something else."

Frankie sighed. "Honestly, it's just my reality. Look, you've already heard enough sob stories from me to last a lifetime."

"And I'd listen to a thousand more if that's what you

wanted to talk about. I like learning about who you are," he said.

"Yeah, well, nobody wants to be a Debbie Downer on their first date. I'm sure there are other stories that you'd find way more interesting.

He slowed down beside a palm tree, gently placing his hand over hers. "I find everything about you to be interesting, Frankie Jones. We can talk about as much or as little as you'd like, but please don't stop on my account."

It was those specific words that solidified the deal. He was into her and made it so obvious she could no longer deny it. But what was she supposed to do with a guy who was leaving in a week? She hadn't been waiting her whole life for a one-week fling; she wanted the real thing.

On the way in through the double glass doors, the front desk crew waved, looking particularly interested in her appearance and the company she was keeping. They still smiled. After a brief wave, she pushed through the crowd while leading Christian across the atrium to their next stop.

She stood in front of the entrance of their finest restaurant. "Since you're not much of a casino kind of guy, I thought I'd switch things up and show you our fine dining. It's the perfect place for a bachelor to take a woman of interest."

Christian stepped up to the window, noticing the menu. "Now, again, this is impressive, but not unique. The competition has five-star restaurants as well. What I want to know is, what separates The Cove from the rest? Why should I, as a bachelor, stay here above any of the other resorts?"

She took a step closer, gently poking his chest. "This is starting to become the most difficult tour I've ever given. I suppose my first task should be to find out what you like to do, then tailor everything accordingly," she teased.

While exposing his dimples, Christian glanced at his

watch. "I have an idea. To make up for being a little difficult, and to help set the atmosphere for a romantic date —"

A flush feeling washed over Frankie as the time registered in her mind. "Is it really two o'clock?" she asked.

He nodded. "On the dot. I was going to suggest we make a reservation for eight. Maybe afterward we can go dancing."

Frankie barely heard the words that he spoke while scrambling through her purse. "I might have to take a raincheck. Actually, I hate to do this, but I might have to cut the date short," she said, finally locating her phone.

After scrolling through a few missed messages, the one from Meg confirmed her suspicions. Parker's party was in an hour and she was nowhere nearly as prepared as she wanted to be.

He stared. "Is it something I said? I know I have a way of inserting my foot into my mouth at times, but I sincerely —"

"Christian. You're fine. It's me. I have a pool party to attend at three, and I guess the time slipped away without me noticing," she said, watching as his facial expression deflated.

She continued. "Poor planning on my part. I thought we could grab a quick breakfast sandwich, hang for a little while, and head back. I didn't anticipate having —"

"Such a good time with one another?" he said, finishing her thought.

The tension released as they both began laughing. She didn't want to leave him, but like any loyal friend, she wasn't going to ditch her friend's party.

Christian stepped forward, planting a subtle kiss on her forehead. "I had a great time with you today. And, if it's not too much to ask, I'd love to see you again this week. Even if it's just to complete our tour."

Frankie shifted, leaning to one side. "I have a better idea," she flirted.

"What's that?" He smiled.

"You feeling up for some more adventure?"

The corner of his lip curled upward. "What did you have in mind?"

"Follow me."

With that, Frankie turned about-face, fully expecting him to follow, and fully expecting to have a good time.

Chapter 8

Meg

Meg balanced bags from the local market while mashing the front doorbell. The front porch was a far cry from the way she'd found it when she met Parker for the first time. With everything so bright and attractive, even she wished the for sale sign didn't have to go up.

With a little under an hour to spare, she'd drop off a few soft drinks and help set up. She had to hand it to Parker. He'd made great sacrifices to be there, but the beach house looked absolutely stunning. Now all he needed to do was locate a buyer and his next project.

Ding dong. She mashed again, triggering the bell while listening to the footsteps approaching the door.

"Hello," a fair complexioned male said, greeting her with a huge smile.

Meg checked the driveway, then looked back again. "Hi. I'm here for the —"

He chuckled, "The pool party?"

"Yes," she said, returning the smile. There was probably

something about her pool attire that gave it away. "Is Parker around?" she asked.

"Yeah, he's out back, but don't worry. I got you covered with the bags. Let me take these from you," he replied and with one swift move, he'd managed to relieve her arms of the extra strain.

Standing almost six-feet tall, with a muscular build, and smelling good, Meg definitely hadn't seen this guy before. If she had, she would've remembered. "I'm sorry. Who are you?"

"Brian. Forgive my manners. I work with Parker to help him access building materials and whatnot. He invited myself and a few of the guys to the crib to celebrate, but sadly he failed to mention a beautiful woman like yourself would be here. What's your name?"

"Meg Carter. I'm Parker's girlfriend."

Just then, Parker showed up beside Brian, giving him a big slap on the back. "That's right, my friend, this lovely lady is taken," he said.

Meg eased inside the foyer, feeling thankful for the smooth introduction from Parker. "I know of another lovely lady who will be joining us this afternoon. And, she's not taken," she replied, then kissed Parker on the lips.

Inside, the guys helped her unpack the drinks. She looked around and saw ice buckets, board games on the table, a makeshift grill ready for cooking, and even party lights around the pool. It was quite the setup.

"You did an amazing job on the house, babe. I came early to help out, but it looks like you have everything under control," she said, watching as Brian joined a few people out back. Through the glass door she was able to wave at Miguel, the contractor who worked side by side with Parker every day.

Parker stretched. "Thankfully, that's what happens when you call in a few favors to the guys. I promised to-go plates for anyone who could show up early and help with setup. My intention was to do it all myself, but after last night's meeting that ran late, I knew there was no way."

Meg turned Parker around and began kneading her hands into his shoulders. She could sense the familiar tension that she often carried around with her at work. "We have a few minutes to spare before more guests start to arrive. Talk to me. What's on your mind?"

"Ahh, it's nothing that can't wait until later," he responded.

"Parkerrrr. I know for a fact if your sister were here she would be able to talk some sense into you. It's not healthy to keep things bottled up inside. By the way, is she coming today? I really want her to meet my friend Frankie."

He nodded. "Yes, Savannah's running late, but she'll be here with the whole crew."

"Good. So it sounds like you have two choices. Tell me what's on your mind or I'll gang up with your sister when she arrives, and between the two of us, you'll have no choice but to confess."

Parker whipped around, torturing her with tickles along her rib cage. Once he stopped, she humbly submitted. "What I meant to say was if you're feeling up to talking about it —"

"Mmm hmm." He smiled. "That's what I thought. Seriously, all jokes aside. Have you ever been offered something larger than your mind can comprehend? I'm talking something unexpected and so big you have a hard time wrapping your mind around it?" he asked, then held her close, giving her a peck on the forehead.

Meg folded her eyebrows. "The only time that comes to mind was when I received the call for the job at The Cove. Even though, as I reflect from then to now, the job isn't as glamorous as I made it out to be in my mind. I guess you have to be careful about how good something appears to be."

"So, do you completely regret accepting the offer?" he asked.

"Yes and no. I'm a hospitality girl at heart. If I'm able to fulfill my dreams of owning a slice of hospitality heaven here on earth, that would be amazing. Let's face it, I love the Bahamas. But, I'm unhappy working with Iris. I feel like her sole purpose in life is to make my life a living —"

Parker placed his finger over her lip. "Sweetheart, I didn't mean to get you all worked up. It's the weekend. A time to relax and forget about work. We can pick up on this conversation later on."

She tugged on the collar of his button-down shirt. "Not before you tell me about this opportunity. Clearly it's eating away at you. What is it?"

Before Parker could reply, the doorbell rang again, making it easy for him to slip away.

* * *

Meg watched proudly as Parker entertained his guests and showed off the main floor of the home. She, on the other hand, pulled up a chair in between his sister and Frankie.

"Ladies, I'm so glad to see you getting acquainted." She nudged Savannah. "Did Frankie mention that we're co-workers and roommates?" Meg asked.

Savannah nodded. "She did. I think it's great that you two are able to save by living together. I'm sure Parker has already shared how expensive it can get out here. Depending on what you're looking for, of course."

Brian pulled up a chair next to Christian, making himself quite at home, although everyone at the table was taken. He scratched his head, giving Christian a puzzled stare. "There's something about you that seems awfully familiar, man. I feel like I've seen you somewhere before. What was your name again?" he asked.

"I don't recall announcing it, but my name is Christian Halstead. Perhaps you saw somebody that looks like me? I'm definitely not from the area."

Brian slouched back, crossing his legs over. "Hmm."

Meg took in the panoramic view of the pool, the beach in the distance, the kids playing, the guests chatting with Parker, and it all seemed so serene. But sadly, the only thing that truly captivated her mind was the continued email notifications that alerted her phone from Iris.

She threw her phone back in her purse and looked at Christian. "Christian Halstead has a nice ring to it. What do you do for a living?" she asked, then winked at Frankie.

"That's a tough question to answer. If I divulge what I do for a living, I could potentially put someone at risk," he replied.

The group paused, seemingly waiting for Meg to probe further. "Well, now you really have my attention."

Brian interrupted. "I really feel like I've seen you somewhere before. Like, on social media or in the newspaper or something," he said, this time seeming almost agitated that he couldn't figure it out.

Christian shook his head. "Again, we all have look-alikes out there, but I highly doubt you've seen me unless you live in Atlanta. And, as for you, Miss Meg, I didn't mean to say anything alarming. It's just, my job requires me to do a lot of undercover work without necessarily being your typical investigator."

Meg nudged Frankie's foot under the table so hard, she practically made her spit her drink out. "Sounds like an interesting line of work, but I should caution you, Mr. Halstead. My friends back at home like to run new guys through a thorough investigation of their own. Just make sure you take good care of our Frankie here. She means a lot to us."

By this point, even Frankie looked dumbfounded by the exchange, but chose not to say anything.

Brian's eyes lit up. "This is bugging the heck out of me. I really feel like I've seen you before —" But by this point Parker was clanging a tin can with a grilling utensil to grab everybody's attention.

Frankie leaned over, whispering in Meg's ear, "Who is that guy?"

Meg smiled, shifting ever so slightly so that only Frankie could hear her. "He's one of Parker's work buddies. A little flirtatious when I first arrived, but seemed nice. I was going to introduce him to you until I realized you had a plus one. By the way, what's with all the secrecy with your guy?"

When the crowd began clapping, Meg saw Parker motioning for her and Savannah to join him by the pool. "Sorry, kiddo, that's my cue. Let's finish this conversation over some food in just a bit," she said, patting Frankie on the shoulder.

Meg followed Savannah then stepped to the side, allowing the two to have their moment. She listened as Parker gave his speech. "Savannah, thank you for being my top designer, extraordinaire. You always add just the right touch to every project we work on. I don't know where this business would be without you."

Everyone clapped as he turned to Meg. "My love," he said, holding her by the hand. "I can remember the moment I met you, just like it was yesterday," he said, closing his eyes. "It was the end of a long day, and I wanted nothing more than to hit the shower and plan for a meeting. With the contract signed and keys in hand, I pulled up this driveway expecting to spend my first night alone."

Meg could feel the adrenaline rush as he retold the story of how they met. He was right. Never in a million years did she expect to spend the night with a stranger. Particularly a stranger she would grow to love.

Parker continued. "But somehow when I walked through the kitchen and saw you, although you were a complete stranger to me, I had a feeling you'd play an important role in my future." He then turned around to face the crowd while holding her hand. "For those of you who don't know the story, I fell in love with this woman right here in this house."

Again, the crowd clapped. Savannah's husband whistled in the background, perhaps influenced by his beverage, but he meant well. She embarrassingly signaled for him to quit.

Meg chuckled. "It's all good, Savannah."

As she turned around, Parker handed over a document, rolled like a scroll with a ribbon tied around it. He handed one copy to her and the other to Savannah.

Parker proudly smiled. "Ladies, if you wouldn't mind doing me the honors. I have a little proposition for the both of you — if you're interested, of course."

In the background, Meg could hear Brian rattling to Christian in the crowd. "I know exactly who you are. You're that reporter guy. You write scathing reviews on major hotel chains. I've read your work before."

Meg held her breath, feeling every ounce of embarrassment for Frankie as his words echoed through the party. Thankfully, most ignored him, keeping all eyes on her and Savannah.

"Well, there's no point in standing here in suspense," she said, unraveling the ribbon.

Savannah spoke first. "A contract for 3009-3012 Seaside Drive. Okayyy. Is this your way of telling me you found your next property? Actually, make that plural because it looks like you found three properties."

Parker nodded. "Keep reading."

Meg couldn't stop staring. If what she was reading was correct, Parker had taken an interest in two B&B properties and a gift shop. *It looked good on paper, but what was he thinking?* she wondered. "I need a little help following along here. Are congratulations in order? Are you going to purchase this place?" she asked.

Parker slid his hands in his pocket. "Before I go into the details, I'd like to make the both of you an offer. Savannah, you've been my sidekick from the onset. If I were to purchase this property, I can't think of a better person to remain on board, helping me with the designs for the B&B, reviving it from the inside out. And, Meg, you've always had a lifelong dream to run a hospitality business, haven't you?"

A burst of nervous laughter slipped out. "Well, yeah, but —"

"No buts. Hear me out on this one," Parker continued. "Instead of working for someone who doesn't appreciate what you have to offer, what would you say if I asked you to join me at the B&B? Not only to help revive an amazing business, but to take one step closer in building our lives together."

Meg listened as he spoke while noticing every hair follicle on his handsome face. Yet she froze, feeling unable to move. When he stopped speaking, she heard nothing but the sound of the pool.

Parker reached out, touching her arm. "Of course, I'm sure you have a lot of questions. Heck, I still have a lot running through my mind." He then looked back and forth between her and Savannah. "I had a chance to check out the property last night, and my initial reaction was total rejection. I mean, this is so far out of my lane. But then I had a chance to look around, and tour the place, and review the numbers, and make a ton of phone calls this morning. Like I said, I can go into the details, but everything I've been through in the last twenty-four hours has led me to this moment."

She watched as Parker shifted his gaze back to her eyes. "And, I thought about you... and us building our lives together, and I .. I dunno. It may be the craziest thing I've ever done, but something came over me this morning. I really think I have a hidden gem here — and while incorporating your knowledge of hospitality, and our property restoration skills..." He nodded towards Savannah. "I think we can all make this work."

Meg could feel the thumping of her heart racing and feel everyone's eyes staring at her. In that moment, all that came to mind was the new book club, and the women sitting around analyzing the life of the lost character, trying to find her way. She could relate to Shelby in the book, feeling just as lost, not knowing what to do.

"Parker," she whispered. "This is a really big decision." Her eyes made contact with Savannah's, then shifted back to his. "One that requires much more than a quick answer in front of a crowd." Meg placed her hand over his, then let it slip away. "I hope you can understand," she said, then quietly excused herself.

Chapter 9

Frankie

"**W**ould you mind telling me what that was all about?" she scoffed, pacing in front of her car. Christian hesitated. "I can explain."

"I sure hope you can. Here I am, taking a leap by inviting you to a friend's house, only to discover that you're some sort of reporter," Frankie argued, releasing a hard sigh. "I guess next you're going to tell me that your name really isn't Christian."

"It is. Everything I've told you about myself so far is true," he replied.

Frankie massaged her temples, trying to remain calm. "Have you ever heard of this thing called lying by omission? Sadly, I know it all too well. It seems to be the story of my life that I end up meeting losers like yourself who are either completely dishonest or who end up walking all over me. But this time, the joke's on you, cause I'm not falling for it."

Christian reached his hands out. "Frankie, listen."

"No, you listen. It's very clear the only reason why you wanted to spend time around me was to pump me for information and use it for your next magazine review or whatever you do. That's pretty low, Christian. Very low. You could've just been straightforward, telling me who you are and what your intentions were. No, that would've been too easy. Instead, you flirt with me, pursue me, and ask me on a date."

"Frankie, I know it doesn't look good, but it's also not what you're making it out to be. I'm not that guy, I promise."

She folded her arms with a look of disdain resting on her face. "Then, by all means, tell me, who are you? Because as of this moment, all I see is a stranger that I got stuck with in the elevator. A stranger I wish I'd never met."

As Frankie observed the look of embarrassment draining his natural color, her mind was consumed with flashbacks of her past. According to her recollection, Daryl, her ex-husband of six months, had made the biggest fool out of her. But there were definitely others.

"Frankie, as I said before, I'm not that guy."

"You are that guy. Now that I think of it, I specifically asked you in the elevator if you were a reporter and you said no. That makes you a liar. Now, how do you explain your way out of that?"

Christian's hands fell to his side. "You're right. There is no explanation for telling a lie. I did it to protect the assignment."

"So, you are writing a review of the resort and using me as your pawn. Great! Jussst great."

"I am writing a review of the resort, but I'm not using you. I genuinely took an interest in you, and that's why I asked you out," he explained.

Frankie rolled her eyes. "Oh, come on, already. Give it a rest. You've been caught in the act, and the least you could do is come completely clean. You were willing to do whatever it takes, even going as far as coming to the pool party just to get some dirt. Everything was about the tour the whole time," she said, waving her hand toward Parker's beach house.

"No. I came here because I wanted to spend more time getting to know you. Think about it, Frankie. I'm the one who suggested that we put off the tour of the resort for another time. I'm the one who suggested that you were hijacking the date, and I'm the one who wanted to make plans for dinner... just the two of us... with no agenda. Do you really think I'd waste my time going out with you just so I can get information for a review? My job paid me to come and stay at The Cove and experience it all for myself. Why would I need you for that?"

The gentle trade wind blew across Frankie's face as she considered his words. She pointed toward the ground as she took a step closer to him. "The way I see things is pretty black and white. You either tell the truth or you don't. And, in this case, if you'd just been honest, then we wouldn't be in this predicament. Thanks to you, I now have the job of explaining all this to my friends. This was completely unnecessary and you should've just been honest. Period."

Back home, Frankie pushed the front door closed with her bottom and just leaned against the door. She could feel the breeze from her ceiling fan twirling and could hear the tranquil sound of her fish tank bubbling in the background. *I should've known better,* she admitted to herself. Her history always had a way of repeating itself, so why would this time be any different? She quietly desired love, but always hid behind a tough exterior so she wouldn't get hurt. And, whenever she stepped out on a limb, the guy always ended up having issues — at least in her experience.

The faint sound of sniffles coming from downstairs distracted her train of thought.

"Meg? Are you okay down there?" she called out.

Frankie kicked off her sandals and eased down the stairs. "Meg?"

"I'm in my room."

Guilt washed over her as she tapped on the door ever so lightly. For a moment she was so caught up in her own drama, she'd forgotten that Meg didn't exactly have a great end to the evening herself.

She knocked softly, then pushed the slightly ajar door further open. "Mind if I come in?"

Meg tossed a pillow at the end of the bed. "Make yourself comfortable."

Frankie stopped. "Meg, what's going on? Why are you down here all by yourself with puffy eyelids?"

"I live here, silly. Where else would I be crying with puffy eyelids?" she said, laughing half-heartedly.

"You know what I mean." Frankie nodded. "I just left the beach house where the most amazing man just offered you an opportunity of a lifetime. Why on earth aren't you back at the party, celebrating?"

Meg gazed down at the floor. "Should I be celebrating, Frankie?"

"What do you mean? Of course, you should be celebrating. I mean, sure, you moved here thinking your job would be at The Cove, but it's not working out and something way better has come along. Isn't this what you've always wanted?"

Meg wiped a tear from her cheek and propped her pillow upright. "What I wanted was to stand on my own two feet and find my own path. And, yes, I also wanted to own a business in the hospitality industry someday. But don't you think if I hit the eject button at The Cove and join forces with Parker that I'm taking the easy way out? And, even worse, I moved here based on the premise that I was sick and tired of following behind a man."

"Meg, this is different. You put your life on hold for a man who didn't love you. He was in a romantic relationship while the two of you were engaged. Parker is nothing like John and doesn't deserve to be put in the same boat."

"I agree, but that doesn't mean that I should be giving up my career and taking this huge leap of faith to be with him. What if we broke up? Who's to say he would want me to stick around? Would I have to start the job-hunting process all over again? I dunno, Frankie. It's a huge pill to swallow and being put on the spot in front of his sister and a crowd of people wasn't exactly the best approach," Meg replied.

"Okay, so maybe he needs to polish up his presentation a bit, but he meant well. Besides, I'm sure this is not the first time you heard him talk about his business ventures and his dreams."

"Uhhh. Frankie, I beg to differ. This whole B&B idea was breaking news to me. Last I heard, Parker was supposed to be moving on to his next renovation. I'm not sure where he got this idea, but there's one thing I know for certain. My whole life has been out of sorts ever since I moved here. I don't know whether I'm coming or going."

Frankie tilted her head downward. "Before you get carried away, let me remind you that you moved here and fell in love. That's not exactly the description of a life that's out of sorts."

Meg paused. "There's no denying that I love Parker. Really, there isn't. But it all happened so fast. I broke off my engagement, accepted a new job, moved here, had another run-in with John —"

Frankie interrupted. "Ugh, do we have to utter his name?"

"Tell me how you really feel." Meg smiled. "We don't have to say his name, but I'm right when I say that everything happened fast. My dad and my stepmother haven't even had a chance to come out and visit me yet. What am I supposed to tell them? *Oh, by the way, I quit my job and started running a*

B&B with this man I fell in love with. Frankie, they don't even know about Parker, for goodness' sake!"

"Well, that's your fault. You better get on it. When are they coming to visit?" Frankie asked.

"Not until the holidays, but still. I know you can see where I'm going with this."

Frankie flopped on the end of the bed, making herself comfortable. "The only thing I see is life trying to take you in a different direction than expected, and instead of you going with the flow, you're resisting."

Meg stared at her nails. "Ouch, do you have to be so harsh?"

"Not harsh. Just speaking the truth in love. You have the right to embrace every blessing that comes your way, Meg. I'm not sure why you're trying to fight it." Frankie paused to prop up on her elbows. "Let's make a deal. Before you make any decisions, talk to Parker. Face to face, one-on-one. Find out what's going on in his head. Then, spend time thinking about it and go from there. No rash decisions in the meantime. Okay?"

Meg took a deep breath. "I think I can handle that," she said, cracking a lazy smile.

"Good, cause any opportunity to get away from Iris is worth looking into if you ask me. Can you just imagine telling her to kiss you where the sun doesn't —"

Meg giggled. "Okay, okay, I get the idea, Frankie. Thank you."

"Just as long as you understand." Frankie laughed.

Frankie reflected back to when Meg moved in, becoming such a dear friend and a really good housemate. At the time, it wasn't what she was looking for, but it was everything she needed.

Meg cleared her throat. "I'll tell you something I need to

understand. What was that whole scene with Brian and Christian all about?"

Frankie buried her head, covering it with a pillow. In a muffled voice, she mumbled, "I don't want to talk about it."

Meg pressed her. "Oh, no you don't. You came down here and made me talk. Now it's your turn."

Frankie persisted. "That's different. I could hear you were upset," she said.

"Frankieeeee," Meg pressed even harder.

"Okay, fine. I found out tonight that Christian writes reviews for hotels and resorts. It just so happens The Cove was his next assignment," Frankie explained. "And if it wasn't for Brian exposing him at the party, I wouldn't have a clue. At least it explains this mystery job he's been avoiding talking about."

"No way."

"Yes, and it gets worse. I believe the only reason he asked me out is because he wanted to pump me for details to help him write the review. Can you imagine him using me like that? And even going as far as hanging out at Parker's place over it, just so he could pretend to be interested in me. Kind of nervy, don't you think?"

Meg wore a puzzled expression on her face. "Frankie, are you sure there isn't more to it? I mean, did you ask him for an explanation?"

Frankie emerged from the pillow, blowing her hair out of the way. "Of course, I did. He swears up and down that his job had nothing to do with his interest in me. But come on, really? I'm sure he just saw me as an easy target that day in the elevator. If you think about it, why wouldn't a woman from HR know all the ins and outs of the resort, right?"

"Wrong! You work in the benefits department, and while you have an extensive knowledge of the place, why wouldn't he just seek out someone from tourist attractions? Or tour the place himself so he wouldn't seem suspicious? He has free rein to roam the place and experience everything for himself. He doesn't need you."

Frankie bit her bottom lip before proceeding further. "None of that matters. He lied, Meg. I came right out and asked him if he was a reporter and he said no," she explained, wiping her hands together. "That, my friend, was all I needed to know. Once a liar, always a liar."

"Was he allowed to talk about the assignment?" Meg asked.

"Hey, whose side are you on?" she asked, feeling passion rising in her veins. "I have scars a mile long from previous liars, cheats, and a drunken ex-husband who lured me here to abuse me. That's enough damage to last a lifetime. I don't need any drama coming from some stranger I just met. If Christian has a problem telling the truth, then he's history. Period."

As soon as the words slipped out, Frankie regretted it. She'd shared a lot about herself, but the ins and outs of her past relationships were where she usually drew the line. Frankie knew the moment she exposed those skeletons, she'd ultimately be admitting to the world that she'd previously been desperate for love, looked in all the wrong places, and even married the bottom of the barrel. *How embarrassing,* she thought.

Meg stuttered. "I — I'm sorry. I didn't realize."

The tense feeling that clenched Frankie's nerves slowly drained out of her system, leaving her empty. "It's not your fault. The poor choices of my past are absolutely no one's fault but my own. As for Christian, you're probably right. I'm sure he was just protecting his job. Sadly, there's a constant voice in my head that won't allow me to fully trust men. So, good guy or not, a lie is a lie. That's my story and I'm sticking to it."

Frankie rose from the bed, smoothed out the covers, and gently returned the pillow. She then stood upright. "You see all of this?" she asked, pointing to herself. "This is what happens when you allow the past to haunt you. Whatever you do, Meg. Don't... be... like... me."

"But —" Meg protested.

But it was too late, Frankie's sights were already set on the bedroom door.

Chapter 10

Parker

Parker cranked the engine to his pickup while Savannah buckled herself in the passenger seat. The two gazed at the road ahead, not speaking a word, but knowing eventually the silence had to be broken. It had already been a long night with minimal messaging back and forth with Meg, so the last thing Parker needed was a lecture from his sister.

Instead, Parker positioned his thermos in his cupholder and shifted the gear into drive. "First stop, Cabbage Beach. According to Old Man Barnes, there's this little B&B off the beaten path he says I should visit. He seems to think it's a great place to get ideas and to observe the overall operation. He's friends with the owner and didn't mind putting in a call so we could stop by."

With the sound of his tires crunching over the grit and pebbles of Seaside Drive, he accelerated and cranked up the music.

"Parker."

"Yes," he replied, already having the sense that a lecture was on the way.

"Have you talked to Meg yet? One would think you'd like to have her along for the ride."

He grunted. "You were there last night. You saw firsthand how well things went when I tried to present the offer to her. And, to answer your question, no, we haven't spoken. We exchanged a few text messages, but that's about it."

Parker could feel Savannah's eyes piercing his skin, but refused to give it any attention.

Obviously picking up on his cues, she continued just the same. "Okay, sooo, maybe I need to make myself more clear. I think you need to have a heart-to-heart with her first before proceeding with this deal. I don't see how you can plan on putting her in charge of hospitality if she's not on board. A decision like this is a very big deal."

He took a sip and nodded. "Indeed, it is, but again, you saw how things went. If push comes to shove, I'll post the position on all the local sites. Surely there's someone out there who'd be grateful for the opportunity."

"Hold on a minute. Surely you're not upset with Meg, are you?"

He glanced at her, then put his eyes back on the road.

"Are you?" she repeated.

"No, I'm not mad. It's totally her call. However, I do think the least she could do was give me a chance to explain further," he said, mashing his thermos back into the cupholder hard enough to splash coffee on his hands. "Ugh, for crying out loud."

Savannah folded her arms. "Pull the truck over."

"What? I'm not pulling the truck over. I spill coffee all the time. It will be fine."

Savannah made a second attempt. "Parker, this has nothing to do with the coffee. Pull over to the beach. I'm still your older sister, and you're not too old for me to occasionally tell you what to do. Now, pull over."

He rolled his eyes. "Savannah, is this really necessary? I have a whole itinerary laid out for the morning, and this little pitstop of yours is going to throw things off."

"Your ability to shut down at a moment's notice is going to throw things off, Parker Wilson, not your itinerary, which can wait."

Some things hadn't changed over a lifetime of being a Wilson. One, if not more, of the women in the family were always determined to set Parker straight if he ever veered from what they thought was right. But this time, he'd gladly pull over and comply. He wasn't the one in the wrong. He'd done a heroic deed. Perhaps he was a little haphazard with how it all came about, but he meant well. All he wanted to do was offer Meg a way out. To him, it was an act of love. So, what on earth was the problem?

He pulled up along Seaside Beach and threw the truck in park. "This better be good, Savannah, because this time I did absolutely nothing wrong."

"Yeah, sure. From your perspective, everything is just peachy. The only problem with that sort of thinking is it's lopsided. Parker, the way you went about this was wrong on so many levels and it was wayyyy out of character for you. Even I was a bit shocked last night and I'm your sister, for goodness' sake. Now, because I know you very well, I'm confident you wouldn't make a business decision that you haven't calculated thoroughly. But does Meg know that? And, while we're at it, how did this deal come about, anyway? I'll always be an automatic yes because you're my brother and I trust you, but even I deserve a few more details. I have kids to feed."

Parker gripped the steering wheel with both hands. "And that's the part that's getting under my skin the most. I expected you two would want to know more. I really did. But you trust me and that's where the rubber meets the road. I'm over here thinking Meg and I are working toward building a life together, but how can we do that if she doesn't trust me?"

Savannah rolled down the window, then audibly breathed in the smell of the ocean. "Men," she exhaled.

"You're seriously putting all of this on me? I'm not the one who walked off in the middle of the party, in case you didn't notice, Savannah."

"Understood, but you put her under a ton of pressure. Why not sit her down privately and explain? Why not paint a picture so vivid for her that when you walked away, all she had to do was envision it for herself and dream? And — biggest one of all. Why not treat her like her name is Meg Carter instead of Jenna Wilson?"

The sharp pierce in his chest cut deep. In a low baritone voice, he said, "What's that supposed to mean?"

"Parker, you and I both know Jenna would've easily hopped on board with practically anything you suggested. And, I believe you are so used to having that kind of relationship with a woman, that you're expecting the same from Meg. She's not Jenna, dude. But it's obvious that she loves you deeply. My suggestion is you sit down and talk to her and then — give it time. It's a much better strategy than having a knee jerk reaction just because your initial approach didn't go as planned." Savannah lowered her voice. "Whatever you do, don't write her off, Parker. Instead, be patient with her."

He ran his fingers through his hair, then leaned back on the headrest. "You're right. I guess I am being a little hasty this morning. Partially because I stayed up all night planning and thinking about everything until the sun came up."

"Mm hmm, and partially because you were disappointed that Meg didn't react the same way Jenna would've."

Parker glanced over. "I hadn't thought of it that way, to be honest. It's not my intention-to treat Meg like she's Jenna. I just had my hopes up that she would be excited, that's all," he explained, with his voice trailing off. "I kinda hoped she would just trust me. Either way, I'll get over it. You can trust and believe I won't let this happen again."

Parker ducked at the sight of his sister reaching to ruffle his hair. It was something she enjoyed doing over the years as they grew up. "Savannah, will you quit already?" He laughed. "I'm not the same little boy you used to tease growing up."

She laughed along. "No, maybe not. But you'll always be my baby brother, no matter how old you get. Besides, you need somebody like me in your life to knock some sense into you every now and again. Meg's a good woman. A really good woman, and from what I can tell, she's been through a lot. Both of you have. The last thing she needs is you being disappointed in her because she's not ready to move at your pace. I'm not sure what it is about men that always want to make everything about themselves. You can't always take everything personally, Park."

This time, he reached for the keys, turning the ignition off. "Don't you think you're being a little harsh?" he asked.

"No. Not at all. Think about it. From everything you've ever shared with me about Meg, it is obvious the woman loves you, but she has a lot going on in her life right now. First there was the breakup. And, yes, we both know she's over her ex, but still. Then she packs up and moves to an island from a big city, then she meets you. And now the two of you are on the fast track to being in love and potentially becoming — more some-day. That's a lot to digest, Park," she expressed, while propping her feet on the dashboard. "I highly doubt her leaving the party early was solely about you. That's all I'm trying to say. Take it from me... I know firsthand because I'm a woman."

Parker looked out of the corner of his eye. If there was one thing his sister was good at, it was usually reminding him of how much of an expert she was. And, although she deserved the credit, he didn't have to be so quick to let her know.

He interjected. "Okay. I hear you loud and clear. Lay off for a little while and let Meg come to her own conclusions without any influence from me. If she wants to reach out and talk to me, cool. If not, be completely understanding and don't press it. I got it. You happy now?"

Savannah playfully shoved his arm. "This has absolutely nothing to do with my happiness. This afternoon I'm going to go home, cook a good meal for the kids, put them to bed this evening, and spend a romantic evening with my husband. If you want to be in the same position with Meg someday, then —"

Parker interrupted. "Okay, I get it. Now, before we miss out on the opportunity to meet this sweet couple and visit their B&B — would you mind?"

"What about Meg?" Savannah asked.

Parker slid his finger around the steering wheel. "I say we put off filling the position and focus on the renovation for now. Barnes has staff members in place that will help to keep things running for the moment, and that hopefully will buy us some time, allowing you and I to do what we do best and Meg time to think about it."

She continued looking at him. "How long before you start seeing a return on your investment?"

"Six months... maybe less," he said, with a little smirk emerging. "It's part of the reason I couldn't refuse. There's no money to put down, the place just needs a little sprucing up, and Barnes is practically signing it over, given that he has no next of kin."

Savannah's mouth dropped. "You're kidding me."

"I couldn't make this up if I tried. I think he took a special liking to me because we share something in common," he said.

Memories of Jenna briefly flashed into his mind. Particularly her love for long walks along any beach they could find, walking hand-in hand. And then thoughts of her love for volunteering. "His wife and Jenna were close, unbeknownst to me. They served together at the local shelter and somehow lost contact when Jenna became ill. And now —" He paused, staring at the hood of the truck. "Now, I get the impression he's tired and longing to be with her again."

Savannah sat upright. "His wife?"

"Yes. You should've heard him, Savannah. He's been running the B&B on his own, but all he could talk about was how things haven't been the same since she passed. He seems lost, like anyone naturally would after losing someone so special. And, to make it worse, he's running low on funds to keep the B&B afloat. He's simply looking for a way out, and believes I'm the right person to take over."

"Unbelievable," she said.

"I know. I refused the deal at first. I took a tour of the place, talked things over with him, and still flat out refused. But something stirred on the inside of me, keeping me up all night long after our meeting. By early the next morning, I got up, continued thinking it through, put in several phone calls, and then I finally opened the envelope."

Savannah unbuckled her seatbelt and shifted to face him. "What envelope?"

"It's in the glove compartment. Take a look for yourself."

Parker watched as his sister reached for the latch, knowing

his life was about to change forever. But he still yearned for more. Deep down, he hoped Meg would also want in just as much as he wanted her in. He hoped that she'd resign, taking a leap toward their future together. But if not, at least he would still have the contents inside the envelope.

Chapter 11

Meg

"Thank you for calling The Cove Resort. This is Meg Carter speaking," Meg answered. With a view of hazy gray skies and storm-like clouds moving across the water, she was glad to be inside, nestled comfortably at her desk.

"Good morning, Meg. It's Mariam. How are you, love?" Meg's heart dropped to the pit of her stomach. It was a precautionary reaction, but Meg suspected in order for her stepmother to dial her number, there had to be something wrong. It's not that they had a bad relationship. One could probably describe it as cordial at best. But the real communication was always with her dad.

"Hi Mariam, is everything okay?"

"Yes and no. I should start by saying we don't want you to be alarmed. Your father was admitted to New York Presbyterian Hospital early this morning, but the doctors already seem to feel pretty confident that he's going to be fine."

Meg took a deep breath. "What happened?"

"Early test results indicate a mild heart attack. However,

you know how stubborn your father can be. He's practically ignoring everything the doctor said and calling it a bad case of indigestion."

"Wow, a heart attack? That's serious," Meg replied.

"It was a mild one, but still enough to leave me out of sorts. Neither one of us saw this coming."

Meg frantically reached for her keyboard to pull up information about the upcoming flights. "Mariam, I'm researching the airlines as we speak. If I can find something leaving Nassau today, then I can be there by this evening."

Meg closed her eyes for a moment, recalling that same panicked feeling washing over her when the phone call came in about her mother. She was a young girl, but old enough to remember like it was yesterday. The rotary phone that hung on the wall in the kitchen had a distinct sound that practically made her jump out of skin. Or perhaps it wasn't the phone that made her nervous, as much as the fear of the doctor calling to say the worst.

"Meg, are you still there?" Mariam asked.

"Yes, I'm here."

"Your father would have a fit if he knew I called you. He begged me not to, but I thought it was only fair."

"Thank you, Mariam. Nothing is more important to me. Dad has always been there for me, so catching a flight out to be with him is the least I can do. Did the doctors indicate how long he might have to stay?"

Mariam paused to blow her nose. "Excuse me. I don't know why I'm reacting like this. The doctor has already reassured me that he's fine. He'll likely be here for a day or so. Not that long. They just need to run a few more tests and monitor him for a while longer. They said his blood pressure was through the roof when we arrived. I don't know what I would ever do if —" her voice trailed off.

"Mariam, dad's strong and he's a fighter. We'll see to it that he changes his diet, or takes whatever medicine they prescribe. Maybe we can try to convince him to retire, because it's long overdue. We'll do whatever we can to ensure this never happens again. But, you have to remember the most important thing of all."

Mariam cleared her throat. "What's that?"

"If God was ready to call him home, he could've done it in the blink of an eye, but he didn't. So, let's try to stay focused on the positive, okay?"

Behind a few sniffles, Meg could hear Mariam agreeing.

"Good. Now, I have my phone by my side if anything comes up, and I'll be sure to send you a message when I confirm my flight."

"Okay."

Meg searched her desk for a pen. "Oh, and one more thing. Please don't tell dad. I'm thinking the less he has to worry about, the better."

"That's a good idea."

Meg dabbed her watery eyes with a tissue while maintaining a strong voice. "Good. I'll see you soon."

After the call ended, Meg completed her research, immediately finding a flight that would leave that afternoon. She figured that would give her enough time to inform Anne, her assistant, run home and pack for the remainder of the week, then catch a cab to the airport.

She grabbed her purse, raised out of her chair, and looked up to the sight of Iris, her boss, coming through the door.

"Where are you headed so early on a Monday morning? I just checked with Anne and she told me your calendar was clear," Iris said.

"Good morning, Iris. I'm actually going to catch a flight to

New York. I just received a call that my father was admitted to the hospital."

Iris reared her head back. "Is he dying?"

Meg could feel a trigger escalate in the lower portion of her gut. "What did you say?"

Without hesitation, Iris replied, "I said, is he on his deathbed?"

A cooling sensation released all over Meg's body. It was the complete opposite feeling she'd always imagined whenever she envisioned telling her off.

Meg thought about it. Then took several steps closer to Iris. "I just told you that my father is in the hospital and that's the only thing you can think to ask me? Who does that?" she said, with a look of disgust on her face.

Iris shifted. "I simply was trying to assess the level of urgency. We just landed a major event for the resort that can bring my sales numbers exactly where they need to be. I'm not about to let anything stand in the way of that."

Meg turned slightly to showcase the office. "Well, by all means, make yourself comfortable. I'd hate for anything like my family emergency to get in the way of your sales numbers."

Iris slipped her hand to her waist. "What exactly are you trying to say?"

"I'm saying that ever since I started working here, you've been unreasonable and extremely rude. But, today — today I've had about all I can take from you, Iris. I wonder what HR would have to say about your level of insensitivity."

"I couldn't care less. I'm not here to make friends, Ms. Carter. I'm highly focused and highly driven. If you don't like it and if you can't keep up with my pace, you don't have to be here."

Meg contemplated her words very carefully. "Hmm, thank you. I think I'll take you up on that offer," she said, handing over the office keys. "Here, these are for you. All the best with your big event."

Meg passed Iris by, confidently walking away while feeling a bit rattled on the inside. *What have I done?* she thought, but continued to walk anyway. After all, it wouldn't be the first time she had to walk away from someone who caused her more harm than good.

* * *

"That woman is cruel and insane. She has literally lost her mind," Meg complained while pacing around terminal B.

"Meg, slow down and take a deep breath," Frankie said. "Your dad needs the calm version of you, not the version that's all wound up and ready to rip Iris a new one."

"I am calm. I'm just aggravated that she would stoop so low. The audacity. The nerve. I mean — What? Is her heart made out of stone? I don't get it," she said, flapping her hands in the air. "You know what? It doesn't even matter. Being with my dad is all that matters at this point. I just want to assure you that you don't have to worry about your rent. The last thing I wanted was for you to hear about this without me at least being able to explain. Especially since I won't be there when you get in tonight. I'll see to it that you have your rent money regardless of my employment status," Meg explained.

"Meg, it didn't even cross my mind. All I want is for you to get to New York safely, be with your dad, and then return safely. The rest we can deal with later."

Meg stared outside, watching a Boeing seven-fifty-seven taxi to the gate. "Frankie," she said in a low voice, "I hope you won't think less of me for saying this."

"Think less of you? I would never. What's on your mind?" she asked.

"I can't help but wonder if this trip and everything going on with my dad is a sign." When Frankie didn't say anything, she continued. "A sign that it's time I head back to New York. I mean — I'd miss Parker, and I would definitely miss you and our friendship. But, things haven't exactly gone as smoothly as planned. From the beach house rental, to Iris and the job, and even our roommate situation." She chuckled. "I was supposed to be a temporary housemate, remember? When we met, you were doing me a favor, showing me the ropes around the job, and giving me a place to stay. But — here I am, months in and I'm backtracking instead of making progress."

"Don't you think you're being a little tough on yourself, Meg? Who says you have to have everything figured out right away?"

Meg's thoughts drifted back to her tenth birthday. She vividly recalled putting on a new dress and pulling her white socks with lace trim all the way to her knees. Her mom unboxed a new pair of black patent leather shoes and gave her the talk about how she was growing up. Those new shoes, coupled with her mother's assurance that one day she'd grow up, get married, and have children of her own... those were the memories that influenced her most.

"My folks always seemed to have life figured out. They made it seem so easy, choosing one career and sticking with it, falling in love so young and staying married for years. I don't know, Frankie. Maybe it was just a different time back then."

"You bet it was a different time," Frankie replied.

In the background, Meg was interrupted by the sound of another call coming in. The screen flashed Parker Wilson.

"Frankie, that's Parker calling on the other line. I'm going to go ahead and take the call before I have to board the plane."

"Sure thing. Take care of yourself and send a message to let me know you arrived safely. The rest we can talk about when you get back, okay?"

"Okay. Thanks for everything, Frankie," Meg responded, then nervously clicked over to the other line. "Hello?"

"Meg, there you are. I've been trying to get through for what seems like an hour. Your assistant told me you had to leave because of a family emergency. Is everything okay?" Parker asked.

A breath of relief eased out as she found an area to make herself comfortable. "Everything will be fine as soon as I can lay eyes on my dad and talk some sense into him about considering retirement. My stepmother called me at work because he was admitted into the hospital for a mild heart attack. They just want to run a few tests before sending him home."

"Man, I'm sorry to hear that, but glad to know he's going to be okay. If he needs specialized care, then at least he's in the right place," he said.

"You're right. But, it's not the hospital care that I'm worried about. If dad's not willing to change his lifestyle, then he's going to have way bigger problems on his hands."

The line fell silent, giving into the sound of the flight announcements in the background.

"Which airport are you flying into?" he asked.

"LaGuardia. I'll arrive just in time to grab a cup of coffee for my Uber ride into the city. Just like the good old days." She chuckled.

In a voice of disapproval, he said, "Hmm. Well, I don't like the sound of you traveling around the city by yourself at night. Please let me know when you get there safely."

"I will."

"Meg, before I let you go, I need to apologize for springing things on you the way I did. My approach wasn't well thought out at all. I was excited, but I should've waited and talked to you when we were alone. I started to, but you know how men can be when they get all wound up with an idea," he explained.

Meg nodded, smiling on the other end of the line as if he could see it. "Yeah, to say you were excited was an understatement."

"I'm sorry, Meg. I really am. And to say that I miss you right now would also be an understatement. I miss you so much and I have so much that I want to share with you — so much to explain. I truly wish I could have a do-over, but honestly, none of that matters right now. All that matters is that you get to spend time with your dad, nursing him back to health. We can always talk about the rest when you get back to the island."

Meg bit into one of her nails. "About that, Parker. I don't know how long I plan to stay in New York. I figured I'd just play things by ear."

"Sure, okay. I understand. You probably want to be there until your dad gets settled in at home. Maybe even a little beyond. By the way, you'll have to tell your dad that I'm praying for a speedy recovery and I can't wait to meet him."

She cleared her throat, knowing she hadn't exactly brought Parker up to her father. Passing along well wishes from an unknown boyfriend might be a little awkward, to say the least. "That's kind of you. But, about my stay. I could be back next week, a couple of weeks from now, or who knows. Maybe even a month. I think I'm going to take a little time to clear my head and figure a few things out. There's nothing like being back home to help give you a fresh perspective," she said, trying to brush it off like it was nothing.

Parker seemed surprised. "A month? Don't you have to get back to the resort?"

"Not really. As of today, I'm officially unemployed. Turns out my boss didn't care for an impromptu trip to visit my sick father. And, since my father will always have priority over someone like Iris... I just left without giving it a second thought. I'm certain it was a combination of emotions running through my veins, but her reaction to my dad — that was the last straw."

Over the P.A. system, Meg could hear the clerk announcing boarding for her flight. She rose to her feet, grabbing her duffle bag while wedging the phone between her shoulder and her ear. "Parker, they're calling my flight for boarding. We'll probably have to pick up with this conversation later on at some point."

In a hurried voice, Parker said, "Meg, I know it may not seem like it right now, but maybe this is all a blessing in disguise. You were miserable working for Iris. Maybe this is an opportunity to come and visit the B&B when you get back. Or at least hear the details and see if it's something you might like to do."

She grunted, but quickly covered it up by pardoning herself among the crowd. "Parker, I thank you for thinking of me. And, I know whatever you decide to do with the B&B, it's going to be a total success. Everything you put your mind to is a success. But I don't know how to respond to you right now. Partially because I don't have the slightest clue about how to properly run a B&B —"

Parker interrupted. "You wouldn't have to worry about that. We're being coached by the best. Mr. Barnes agreed to stick around for a while and show us the ropes. And, he's also teaming us up with another couple I met today who run their own B&B. That in conjunction with your hospitality experience and a ready-made staff, I really don't see how we can go wrong. Plus, Savannah and I still get to do what we love best, which is taking old things and making them new. It's a win-win no matter how you slice it."

She took a deep breath, counting at least three more people ahead before she had to end the call and scan her ticket.

"Parker, I'm glad that you found something that you can be so over the moon about. I really am, but —"

He interrupted again. "I'm over the moon about you, Meg. Not just this opportunity, but about us, giving it a go, and beginning a new chapter of our lives together."

It was those very words that melted her heart the most. Especially given with what she was about to say. "I understand, but I need time. I need to figure out what I'm doing with my life first before I can make such a huge decision. Call it bad timing, but if you truly care about me Parker, then you'll understand that right now I need to focus on dad and clearing my mind. At this moment, that's about all I can handle."

"Sure. I understand," he said, clearing his voice.

After those words were spoken, she reached the front of the line, handing over her ticket. "I hate to get off so abruptly, Parker."

In a somber voice, he said, "It's okay. I understand you have to board. Just send me a message when you arrive. The rest we can talk about some other time."

"Thank you."

Meg stared at the screen before mashing the end button. It felt like the conclusion of one of the most difficult conversations she'd had since arriving on the island.

Chapter 12

Frankie

Frankie pulled a beach hat off the shelf, trying out the new look in front of a mirror. She'd taken the day off and traded her HR duties for a nice stroll at the local marketplace. It was a quiet Tuesday, and she couldn't think of a better place to be alone while working on reviving her casual attire.

Maybe she'd grab something for lunch or go back home and do absolutely nothing, but for now she'd shop and treat herself to a day without a care in the world.

"Hey there," the deep sound of a man's voice said as she returned the hat to the shelf. She glanced over her shoulder, noticing Christian.

You have got to be kidding me, she thought to herself. "Hi."

He pointed toward the hat. "I wouldn't be so quick to put that one back. The color looks amazing on you, and the polka dots add a nice flare to the design," he said.

In a direct tone, Frankie replied, "I actually think the hat is rather ugly," then brushed past him, moving on to the next aisle. A few feet behind, she could hear him mumble under his breath, "Okay."

She looked up. "Let me guess. I guess I'm supposed to believe you just happen to be here on the same day, at the same time as me. Or would a better guess be that you're really here spying on me in hopes you'll get some dirt for your review?"

Frankie hadn't spoken to Christian since the party, but it was clear her feelings were still hurt. Even she was surprised by her own reaction.

Christian followed her to the dresses. "I would never spy on you. My assignment involves writing a review of the resort, not you."

Her eyebrows raised. "Well, one can never be too sure. It's not like you have a history of being honest with me," she replied.

Frankie could feel Christian passing her by, positioning himself in front of the rack. He placed his hand strategically over the hanger she was about to pull. "I think we need to talk."

Her eyes widened. "No, we don't. I'm pretty clear on what you're all about. As far as I'm concerned, we're good. The best thing to do is to act like nothing ever happened," she said, trying to step past him.

Christian shifted himself, stepping in her way. "Frankie, I can understand you being upset, but I wasn't supposed to talk about the assignment. Other than that, everything I told you about myself is true. My name is really Christian Halstead. I really live in Atlanta, although I travel for work," he said, digging in his rear pocket and pulling out his wallet. "I can prove it. Here, look at my driver's license."

Frankie relaxed her stance. "Christian, I don't want to see your license."

"Please, look at it anyway." Then he held up the tattoo on his wrist. "These initials I told you about, A.H. They really stand for Allison Halstead, my sister who died in a tragic car accident. You can even look up the incident in the Journal Constitution if it will make you feel any better," he explained.

She did a double take. "A bit morbid, don't you think?"

"I'm not trying to be. But, if you fact check everything I've been telling you, you'll discover I'm not the guy you think I am."

Frankie let out a long breath, noticing a woman, one aisle over, soaking up every bit of their conversation.

Her eyes shifted back to Christian. "Even if I did fact check everything you're telling me, what does it matter now? We chatted in the elevator to pass the time, shared a meal together, and attempted to enjoy a pool party, but clearly it didn't work out. Soon, you'll be on a flight back to Atlanta, I presume. Sooo — what would you like me to do with this information again?"

Christian slid his hand cautiously up her cheek, relieving her from every ounce of tension. "I want you to believe me, Frankie. You can't deny there's something here. Please. Let's not spoil it over something I couldn't control."

She watched as he carefully approached her face, making slow movements closer toward her lips. Feeling awkward yet somewhat weak, she whispered. "So, we're supposed to just kiss and pretend like —"

Frankie felt his finger gently rest over her lip, followed by a sweet shushing sound. It amazed her that he didn't care who was watching. This man was bold and courageous, and was going after what he wanted, which she found to be kind of attractive.

He spoke up. "I don't want to pretend. I want another chance to go out with you and to show you who I really am. This time, just the two of us, and no talk of the resort. I promise not to utter one word about it. What do you say?"

She hesitated, partially because she was thinking about it,

and partially because all her mind could consider was the kiss that almost happened.

He removed his finger. "Please? Can I pick you up this evening, around eight?"

Frankie straightened herself out while again noticing not one, but two people being fully entertained by their conversation. The original woman wore a smirk on her face while pretending to shop. The second one stood with her mouth open wide enough to catch a fly.

Frankie refocused. "Fine. With one exception."

"Sure, anything. Just name it," he said.

"I'll drive myself. Where do you want me to meet you?"

He looked down. "Uh."

She smiled, remembering he was a tourist and not a local. Although she didn't expect much to derive from the outing, the least she could do was help him out and make a suggestion. "How about the Stoned Crab? You know, the restaurant you mentioned earlier."

He smiled. "Yes, I know it well. But I thought you said you've already been before."

"There are not many places you could take me on this island that I haven't been. I'm the adventurous type. I like to explore," she said.

"Really? In that case, what are you doing for the rest of the week?"

She scoffed at him. "I'm working. You know, that thing that most people do Monday through Friday unless they're retired or independently wealthy."

He chuckled. "You have a good sense of humor, I see. But, if work is such a concern, how come you're not there today?"

"There's nothing wrong with taking a mental health day every now and again."

He nodded. "Mmm, well, how about I make you a deal?

Since you like adventure, and I like adventure, why don't we spend the rest of the week together and make the most of our time before I head back to Atlanta?"

Frankie returned to the racks, trying desperately to focus on each article of clothing. "I'm taking my chances by going out with you tonight, but a whole week? Now, you're pushing your luck, buddy."

Christian quickly apologized. "Okay, I don't mind starting slow. I just want to get to know you better and show you who I really am. Sooo, how about tonight at eight? Why don't you meet me at the boardwalk near Stoned Crab? We can grab something to eat, maybe listen to a little music, and talk. How does that sound?"

She could hear Meg's voice gently nudging her in the back of her mind, encouraging her to be more forgiving. After a brief hesitation, and a mental note that she had the power at any time to call it a night, she agreed to go on the date.

* * *

At the dinner table, Frankie's heartbeat leapt in unusual patterns as she watched Christian signal for the check. Maybe it was his mannerisms, his muscular build, or even his Hawaiian print shirt that made him look so good. She didn't know what it was, but she tried desperately to focus on something more productive. "How did you know that I would be at the Marketplace earlier today?"

Christian smiled. "I didn't know. Call it fate, but I was out for a much needed break. Now that my work is behind me, I'm spending the last few days on vacation and truly am out to explore."

"Ahhh. So, when you say your work is complete, does this mean you wrote your review of The Cove?" she asked.

"I thought we agreed no talk about work?"

She folded her arms. "So, you are keeping secrets? I knew it."

"No, that's not what it means at all," he said, reaching across the table. "If you want, I'll tell you everything. I did write a stellar review focusing on the wonderful amenities The Cove has to offer for families and singles alike. I raved about the golf course, restaurants, nightlife, and more. And, I also talked about the amazing staff, who go above and beyond, even if it's beyond their call of duty," he explained.

Frankie nervously held the edge of her seat, hanging on to his every word. "Really?"

"Yes, really. Again, as I promised from the start, I have nothing to hide other than my boss prefers for me to keep a low profile so I can seek out the most organic experience and write about it. That's all."

"Oh," she said, feeling humbled, and even a bit embarrassed, at how she carried on after the party.

Christian paid for the bill, then reached back, taking her by the hand. "Can I be transparent with you about something?"

"Sure."

"I hate first dates, and even second dates, for that matter. There's always that awkwardness that comes with judging if you're saying too much, or too little, or doing something to scare the person away."

Frankie laughed. "I think you did a pretty good job with that one already."

"My point exactly. I'm as nervous as I can be tonight because I don't want to say or do anything else to make you want to leave. I really like you, Frankie. And I was hoping we can just pretend like this was date number twenty so we can just enjoy each other and have a good time." He smiled.

Feeling at ease, she said, "So far I don't think you have

anything to worry about. We made it through dinner, didn't we?"

"We did. And on that note, would you like to join me for a walk?" he asked.

Frankie placed her hand securely in his. "Lead the way."

Outside, she stepped rhythmically over to the sultry tunes of a live band playing nearby. The traditional Bahamian music had a way of touching her soul and making her feel free. "Do you like to dance?" she asked.

"I'm not sure if what I do is called dancing, but if you move slow enough, and promise not to hurt me, I think I'll be able to keep up," Christian replied, taking her arm and placing it on his shoulder.

With her heartbeat being rhythmically challenged by his masculine touch, she again tried desperately to stay focused. "Tell me something."

"Okay."

She lowered her voice. "What should two people talk about by the time they've reached their twentieth date?"

As they danced cheek to cheek, she could feel him smiling. "By the twentieth date, I'd like to think the couple would be very familiar with one another. They've shared everything about their families, growing up, likes and dislikes, you name it. All the cards are on the table. No holding back."

She paused, looking him in the eyes. "You're leaving Friday. That's darn near impossible to achieve, Halstead."

"Not when you really desire to know everything about a person," he said.

Frankie felt as if everything around her began fading into the background. The people disappeared, the music, the atmosphere; it was almost as if she and Christian were dancing all alone. "Okay then, Mr. Twentieth Date. Why don't you start? Tell me everything there is to know about Christian Halstead."

He dipped her playfully, then pulled her back to dancing cheek to cheek. "Hmm, let's see. I was born and raised in Athens, Georgia, but spent quite a few years living in Atlanta. Most say I lost my southern accent not long after I started traveling. If you ask me, I think I sound the same."

Frankie, you cannot fall for this guy, she thought. "Yeah, I get that a lot myself after leaving the UK. I lived with my cousin in New York for a while, and here in Nassau, so if anything, I probably just confuse people." She laughed.

He stopped her. "There's one thing I'm definitely not confused about. You are a very attractive woman, inside and out," he said, gently locking his fingers between hers.

Her eyes drifted away. "Why, thank you. But I'm sure you might think differently of me if you knew everything about me."

Christian slowed down the rhythm of their dancing even further. "Try me."

Looking off into the distance, she said, "What do you mean, try you?"

He cleared his throat. "You can't scare me away, Jones. I'm already hooked. Besides, what do we have to lose? Becoming vulnerable and sharing the very depths of who you are can oftentimes be very therapeutic."

Frankie's hip swayed to the left as she considered what he was saying. "I don't know what kind of organization you work for. The last thing I need is to have my business plastered all over this week's news," she teased, but deep within, she was also serious.

Christian pulled away and took his cellphone out, tapping the keys and scrolling.

"What are you doing?" she asked.

"Proving to you once and for all who I am and what I really do for a living. Here, look for yourself." He passed the phone over. "Scroll through everything. Look at my title, click on some of my sample work. We can go sit on a bench while you look at everything."

She stood in place, searching through the website. That's when it hit her. Once again, Frankie Jones was about to get in her own way, allowing mistrust and past experiences, even trauma, to provoke skepticism instead of trust.

"Here," she said, passing the phone back.

"No, read it through. I want you to feel comfortable with me."

"I don't need it, Christian. I believe you. Truth be told, the way I'm acting has nothing to do with you. I'm sure you're a phenomenal guy, but there are so many layers to me than what you see on the exterior. I'm almost certain you wouldn't want to pursue me any further if you really knew the truth."

Christian reached out to her. "Again, you won't know unless you try. How can you ever discover true happiness if you won't let anybody in?"

"You're leaving in a few days," she said.

He tilted her chin upward. "Try me."

Feeling all the passion rising up over the thought of missing out on a normal life, she finally spilled over. "I've been lied to, cheated on, and slapped around so many times I could hardly think straight. And, to this day, the only one who knows about it is me. Actually, myself and the judge who granted my annulment, but even he turned a blind eye to certain things. Not exactly something one would want to share on their second date, but since this is our twentieth —" she said, holding up quotation marks in the air. "And, since you wanted to know me so badly, there you have it. It doesn't get any more transparent than that." She started to turn around. "Oh, and let's not forget the whole elevator scene — being trapped in a dark box was nothing but a reminder of the abuse and trauma I experienced with my ex-husband. I couldn't escape from that elevator fast enough, just like I couldn't get away from him fast enough, either."

In Frankie's mind, that was it. She'd done it. She let all her skeletons hang out for him to see and did it with ease, knowing he'd be leaving in a couple of days.

She broke the silence with a chuckle. "Bet you didn't see that coming, did ya?"

Christian gingerly approached her, taking both of her hands. "Frankie, I can't make light of something like this. It breaks my heart to think some coward would do this to you."

Looking into his eyes, she replied, "You don't have to worry about me. It's been a few years now since I left him and moved on with my life. But, it's the very reason why I'm divided. A part of me wants love again, and the other part is very cautious. I was so vulnerable back then. I wanted love so badly that I darn near fell into the arms of the devil. I won't travel down that road again."

She watched as Christian searched her eyes. It felt like he was searching her soul. "But what if you met someone who could help you through the process of healing? Someone who could love you the right way, proving every day that he's not out to hurt you, but to love you," he said.

"That's a big 'what if'."

He grunted. "Make a statement like that to Mary Halstead, and she'd set you straight real quick."

"Excuse me?"

She didn't know who Mary was, but she knew his tone needed to be set straight.

Christian began strolling down the boardwalk, giving her a signal to follow. "Mary Halstead is no longer living. She's my mother. She passed away the year I graduated from college. However, when I was at the tender age of twelve, she too was the victim of being married to a man with a heavy hand. That man was my father, Newman Halstead. You can only imagine what life was like at twelve, jumping in front of your father to block him from hitting your mother. It happened countless times and there was nothing me or my younger sister could do about it."

Frankie gasped and covered her mouth.

He continued. "Mary endured his abuse for years. And no one we grew up with knew a thing about it. None of our family members, or so I thought, and none of our neighbors. But you know what, Frankie? The day Mary decided she'd had enough, she'd really had enough. It was like she flipped a switch. Was she still broken? Yes. But I watched her pack our belongings, move us to Atlanta, and start her life all over again."

"Did she have a support system? Friends or family to help her?" Frankie asked.

"No, she just had us kids. It was a struggle for a while. But, eventually, she was able to get back on her feet, making a life for herself again. I won't stand here and pretend like it was easy. But she even went on to remarry again." He paused, gently grazing her arm. "The key is, she knew she deserved a better life, and she got up one day and decided to make it happen."

Frankie thought about what he said. She'd spent so much time working on her tough exterior, putting up protective guardrails.

"Wow, my one year disaster of a marriage is nothing in comparison to what your mom went through," she said.

Christian placed her hand in the palm of his. "There's no comparison. The real question is, have you considered what you deserve? And, are you willing to tear down those walls inside, and make room for somebody to love you the right way?"

She contemplated, then looked him in the eye. "Christian, even if I was ready, why do you care? Nassau International has a ticket waiting with your name on it."

"This doesn't have to be my last trip to the island, you know," he whispered in her ear.

She could practically feel the stubble from his beard as he grazed toward her lips. He'd come as close as he could but slowed down, waiting as a gentleman should.

Her voice cracked. "We're just fooling ourselves if we think—"

"Stop thinking for a moment and just feel," he whispered, moving in even closer.

She gave in, easing her lips onto his, receiving his tender kiss.

Chapter 13

Meg

"**D**ad, I didn't come here to argue. I'm your daughter, and I have the right to be concerned," Meg pleaded, easing onto his bedside.

"Honey, I thank you for being concerned, but I really wish Mariam would've told you to stay home. Don't let the hospital gown fool you. I'm fine. Perfectly fine," he replied.

"If that's the case, why are you still here?"

His smile slowly drooped. "According to the doctor, they're running test after test, just to be certain. You know how it is. They'll do anything to drive the bill through the roof before they release you."

Mariam interrupted. "Sweetheart, New York Presbyterian has a wonderful reputation. If we're really being truthful, you've had a history of health issues in the past. They need to run all the tests they can. Have you forgotten about the surgery you had three years ago for your clogged arteries?"

He patted his belly. "I have a fond relationship with food. What can I say?"

Meg listened as they bantered back and forth. It was their

usual way, exchanging passionate conversation, seasoned with love, of course. However, it still didn't negate the fact that her father's health needed a little TLC.

"Okay, you two. I'm not here to get in the way or add any stress. I'm just worried about you, Dad, that's all. Over the couple of weeks, I don't care if I have to wait on you hand and foot. I'll do anything to ensure this doesn't happen again."

Samuel Carter propped himself upright in the bed, appearing to be agitated by all the cords and monitors. "The next few weeks? Honey, as much as I love the idea of you visiting, how can you stay away from your new job that long? I have a stack of papers a mile high waiting for me back at the office."

"About that, Dad. I realize now is not the time to discuss this, but it may be time to start thinking about retirement. It's long overdue and probably the very reason we're here today."

His eyebrows perched upward. "At this rate, you may as well put me in a nursing home."

"But, Dad, I —"

"No. Now, it's my turn to speak. You and Mariam have been very gracious, always taking good care, and always wanting the best for me. But, I've already told you once before. If I retire, I wouldn't know what to do with myself. You may as well bury me at that point. My job gives me purpose and besides that, I'm not tired. Only I can make a decision like that and not anyone else."

Meg's eyes wandered to his tray of untouched food as he continued giving his speech. Once he settled down, she made a second attempt in a softer voice. "I don't mean any harm, Dad. I'm just trying to look out for you, that's all," she said, grabbing his hand.

He chuckled. "That's the same face you used to give me when you were little and you knew you were in trouble."

Meg watched as he grabbed Mariam's hand and simultaneously took hers. "I love the both of you, and I know you'd do anything in the world for me. But I'm going to be just fine. Please stop worrying about me and let's patiently wait to hear from the doctors." He smiled.

Mariam kissed him on the forehead. "All right, dear. I'm going to go downstairs and stretch my legs for a little while. Can I get you anything?"

"How about my clothing? There's something about this open gown that feels a little airy, if you know what I mean."

Both Mariam and Meg laughed. "Sweetheart, I think we have to wait until you're discharged. Meg, would you like anything?"

"I'm good, thank you."

Once Mariam was gone, Meg noticed her dad looking at her in the most inquisitive way.

Folding his arms together, he said. "So, you must have a pretty understanding boss to allow you to come and stay for a couple of weeks," he emphasized. "That's kind of unheard of in a new job, isn't it?"

Meg's eyes shifted to the bedspread. "Yes, isn't that something? I guess things are really starting to shift in today's job market. They're really understanding the need for work-life balance and the importance of family care."

Resting his folded arms on his belly, he replied, "Mm hmm. Meg, what's really going on with you? You were never a good liar as a little one, and you still aren't a good liar today."

She sighed and then hesitated. "Dad —"

He held her chin up. "Talk to me, Meggy. I know you're here because you care, but I also can tell something's not right with you. Is it the job? Are you having problems with your roommate?"

"No, no. Everything is fine with Frankie. She's been such a godsend, allowing me to stay at a reasonable rate and just being a supportive friend. I couldn't ask for a better living situation," she replied.

He leaned back again. "Then, is it the job?"

She nodded, feeling somewhat childlike as she feared his opinion. "I quit."

His eyes widened. "You did what?"

"I know what you're going to say, Dad. Under normal circumstances, I would plan for something like this. The same way I did when I left New York. But the woman I worked for — she was ruthless. It's no excuse, but I'd had it with her, and after her last comment, I lost my temper and quit."

It amazed her just how much she still sought her father's approval, even though she was grown. She didn't know why, but what her dad thought meant the world to her.

He slowly smiled at her. "Oh, baby girl," he said, nodding his head. "You are definitely your mother's child. A true Taurus at heart. If only she were still here to see you now. She used to get all fired up and passionate over various matters, and I swear on everything I own you are the same exact way. If you went as far as quitting, this boss of yours must've really struck a nerve," he said.

"It's been a buildup of unreasonable requests, but for me, the icing on the cake was —"

She thought better of it. Her dad really didn't need to hear Iris' thoughtless words, the same way she really didn't need to repeat them. "I just don't think it was a good fit for me, that's all."

He adjusted himself, resting on the pillow. "Well, you know how the saying goes. When life gives you lemons, make lemonade. When you get back, start putting your feelers out there by applying to other hotels. I'm certain somebody will recognize just how talented and valuable you are."

Meg's thoughts flashed to Parker.

"Meg?" her dad asked.

"Sorry. What were you saying?"

"Is everything else okay on the island?" he asked.

"Sure, everything's fine."

He gave her a look. One she'd seen a thousand times whenever he knew something was up. "Well, maybe not everything, but nothing I can't figure out. Besides, I didn't come here to focus on me. Your health is what's most —"

"Meg Carter," he said in a stern voice.

"Dad, you look thirsty. I think I'm going to refill this pitcher and look for the doctor while I'm at it," she said as she rose from the bed.

"Meg, will you have a seat, please? You're not too old for me to put you over my knee, you know," he teased. "Clearly, we have some catching up to do. Now, are you going to allow me to lie here, staring at the walls, while wondering what's going on in your life, or are you going to tell me?"

She nervously shook the pitcher of water. "I met someone."

An instant look of relief washed over his face. "It's about time." He laughed. "I was hoping you wouldn't allow John to leave a permanent scar, preventing you from moving on. Who is he? Tell me all about him."

Feeling heat rising in her face, she said, "His name is Parker. He renovates homes, and he's from Chicago. We've been dating for a little while now, and things are going rather well."

"That's amazing, Sweetheart. How did you two meet?"

She reflected. "The short version... he purchased the beach house I was originally renting. Not to bore you with the details, but we kind of hit it off and kept in touch. From that point on, things have blossomed rather nicely."

In that moment, Meg realized she needed to stop worrying about receiving her dad's approval on every little thing. He'd already proven he'd love her unconditionally. Therefore, it was time for that mindset to go.

"Is it serious?" he asked.

She took a deep breath. "I'm in love. We're both in love. But I keep getting this feeling deep down inside that our timing may not be right."

"Sweetheart, what do you mean? There's no such thing as perfect timing. It doesn't exist."

"I know, Dad, but hear me out," she said, as she started pacing around the room. "What if I fell in love, but I'm really not ready? I mean — look at the way things fell into place. Not long ago, I was preparing to walk down the aisle with John until things went south."

Samuel interrupted. "Really, Honey? Did you really believe you two were going to make it down the aisle after he put off the wedding for three years?"

Her mouth dropped open. "Touché, but still, my heart was in it even if his wasn't."

"Mm," her dad responded.

"I packed up the apartment, left my job, and moved across the ocean to the Bahamas. Sometimes I have to stop and pinch myself to see if it was really all a dream. What if I moved too quickly? What if I'm supposed to be back here in New York, making a life for myself in the city? I mean, after all, I'm a city girl, born and raised. Do you think I may have set my sights too high?"

Again, her dad chuckled, jiggling his belly wholeheartedly. "I'm actually glad you showed up. This is way more entertaining than listening to these beeping monitors."

"Dad, I'm serious." She smiled.

"I know. Go on. Tell me more about this horrible life you're living in the Bahamas, where you get to watch beautiful sunsets and live by the beach."

Meg raised her hand over her hip. "Ha ha, don't think for one minute I don't see what you're doing."

"Okay, all jokes aside. Continue, I'm all ears," he said.

"There's not much more to tell." She hesitated. "Well, technically, that's not true. Parker stumbled upon an amazing opportunity to purchase a B&B property and fix it up. He wants me and his sister to come work with him, but I figured that can be kind of dicey, being that I'm still trying to figure out what I want to do with my life."

There, she'd finally said everything. She let it all hang out. Her whole life, every emotion, every thought, was hanging out there in full transparency for her dad to inspect. The real question was what would he have to say about it?

He gazed at the blank television screen. "Should I remain quiet, or do you want my opinion?"

"Of course, I want your opinion. What you think matters to me," she said.

"Good. I think you're being foolish."

Meg watched as her dad folded his arms again in protest. "Soo — you don't think I left New York in haste? Let's face it, I immediately applied to jobs trying so hard to get away from John that I ended up leaving behind the people I love most."

"Honey, listen to me. You didn't leave to get away from John or from us. You left to finally start pursuing your dreams. The same dreams that were deferred while he kept you waiting on the sidelines for three years. Remember?" he asked.

Meg nodded. Her father was right. Everything she ever wanted in life was placed on the backburner to be supportive and make her man happy. And what did she receive in return? A pink slip and a notice that another woman had taken her place.

She grunted. "Yes, I remember."

"Good. Now, regarding your career, I would pursue whatever makes you happy. Whatever you're passionate about doing for a living. You're the one that has to get up and be satisfied with the work you do every day. No one else. And one more thing. Please promise me you won't go around saying that you left us behind. I certainly don't feel that way and neither does Mariam. We're thrilled for you, and all we want is to see you succeed."

Meg smiled. "Thanks, Dad."

"Don't thank me just yet. I still want to hear more about this new guy of yours. Is he good to you?"

She nodded. "So good sometimes I have to pinch myself to make sure he's real."

"Mmm. And this job opportunity of his. Does it fall into alignment with your goals?" he asked, crinkling his brows.

"I haven't heard all the details yet, but I believe it will put me on the path to entrepreneurship. Something I've always dreamed of."

She noticed her dad pausing deep in thought before asking the following question. "And, you're certain that he genuinely loves you?" he asked.

Just then, the doctor knocked on the door, interrupting their conversation. It was just as well. Most days she thought she was sure about everything, and other days she was certain about absolutely nothing.

"Is your dad going to be okay?" Casey asked on the other end of the telephone line.

Meg turned on the burner under the teakettle, hoping to make herself useful.

"He's nestled in his bed for now. We'll see how long that lasts. The hospital discharged him early this morning, giving him orders to spend the rest of the week taking it easy. He also has new medication to take which he absolutely detests. Other than that, there's nothing else they can do." Meg rolled her eyes. "He's already given Mariam and me strict orders not to wait on him hand and foot. So for now, she's taking care of the laundry and I'm keeping busy in the kitchen. I guess we'll just have to play it day by day," Meg explained.

"Aww, your poor dad. Tell him I'll be praying for a speedy recovery."

"Thanks, Case. I will. So, how's the pregnancy coming along? And how's Craig and the kids? I feel like it's been a while since we had a chance to catch up."

As young girls, Meg and Casey had dreams of doing everything at the same time. Getting married, buying a big house to live in, and having enough kids to count on two hands. Fortunately, it was working out for Casey. Meg's plans, on the other hand, were derailed.

"Let's see, I finally made it past the throwing up stage, so that's always a plus. I actually feel like getting out of bed and getting dressed, so I guess we can count that as a win as well. Thankfully, Craig has been amazing with the kids or else I don't know what I would've done."

Meg rummaged through the pantry, searching for honey, among other things. "I wouldn't expect anything less from him."

"How about you? How's things going with Parker?" Casey asked.

In order to avoid getting into the weeds over the phone, Meg kept it light. "It's going well. I'll have to bring you up to speed on everything. We should probably get together while I'm in town."

"I'd love that. Just name the day and I'll be here."

"Sounds good, Case. I'll call you soon," she replied.

Meg disconnected the call, realizing an impromptu visit to the store would be very necessary.

* * *

Meg tossed a jar of salsa in her basket before perusing the rest of the international aisle. In true New York fashion, the store was hustling and bustling with folks everywhere. Some navigated the items on sale, while others voiced their opinion about the high prices. But most were on a laser-focused mission to complete their shopping.

In the midst of her observations, a male voice resounded from behind. "Meg?"

Startled, she turned around to the site of John standing beside a dark-haired woman, wearing a peacoat and high heels.

"I thought that was you." He smiled.

If there were ever a moment where Meg could've pretended to be hard of hearing, it should've been then. People did it all the time when they didn't feel like being bothered. But, instead, she stood there fighting a sudden bout of nausea.

"John. Hi," she said, forcing a fake smile.

He hesitated, then came toward her with open arms, causing his lady-friend to raise a brow. "What are you doing in New York?" he asked.

Meg responded, stiffly enduring the hug before she withdrew. "My dad was in the hospital. I'm here to spend time with him."

"I'm sorry to hear that. What happened?" John asked, just as if they were old friends from the block.

Meg couldn't help but wonder why the sudden concern. The last time she'd seen him was on the whimsical trip he'd made to the island, begging for her forgiveness. He tried his best to use his sudden illness as a ploy to get her back. And, when it didn't work, she hadn't heard a word from him since.

"He had a mild heart attack. The doctors seem to think if he can focus on exercising and watching his diet, he'll be just fine."

The awkwardness of John's gaze made her look toward the dark-haired woman, then back at him again.

John turned around. "I'm sorry, forgive my manners. Meg, this is Sheila. Sheila, meet Meg Carter, my —"

An internal voice in Meg's mind was having a field day, thinking this moment couldn't be more epic. He'd been better off passing the aisle, pretending not to see Meg, than to stand here and have to introduce her as his ex."

He stuttered. "Meg and I go way back." He laughed nervously.

Coward, Meg thought. A sudden impulse propelled her to step forward, extending her hand toward his attractive companion. "Hi, Meg Carter, John's ex-fiancé. It's so nice to meet you."

Without looking at John, she could feel him trying to maintain his posture. She then turned back to address him. "Gosh, John. It's been a minute since we last ran into each other. What was it? Maybe two months ago when you flew out to the island to ask me to be by your side? How did everything turn out with your health scare?"

The dark-haired woman's mouth flew open wide. Meg knew John well enough to interpret his look of disdain, but she ignored it and continued waiting for a response.

He cleared his throat. "Yeah, about that. Turns out the doctors made a mistake. They've given me a clean bill of health, approving me to get back to my normal day-to-day life."

Meg glanced again at the innocent young lady standing beside him, feeling sorry for what she had to endure. "I see you didn't waste any time. Glad to hear that all is well for you."

With his skin-tone turning three shades of red, John retreated to their cart. "It was good running into you. Please send my regards to your dad. Wish him a speedy recovery for me."

Meg nodded. Then she acknowledged Sheila. "It was nice meeting you." But the only response Sheila gave was a half-hearted attempt at a smile.

Meg took four confident steps away, then slowed down altogether. "Wait a minute. Who does he think he is?" she murmured.

A thrust of emotions she realized still existed emerged, rearing its ugly head right in the middle of aisle five. Meg hesitated, then mustered up the courage to walk right back up to John, tapping him from behind.

He turned around with widened eyes. "Meg?"

"You have a lot of nerve," she announced.

"Hold on a second. I was just trying to be friendly and say hello. No harm, no foul. Right?"

She checked around as if her hearing had failed her. "Wrong, John. You're dead wrong. Knowing you have caused nothing but harm and foul, but not to worry. I will not make a scene in the middle of the grocery store over it. I just think it's pretty presumptuous of you to walk up to me all casual and nonchalant, as if you actually give a darn. Everything about you is vile. You're a self-centered, compassionless pig, with a rotten heart, and frankly, I want absolutely nothing to do with you ever again."

"Hey, I tried to right my wrongs and come after you, Meg. You turned me away in the end. That's on you, not me."

By this point, his lady-friend looked at him as if he had a horn growing out of his head.

"That's a pretty nervy statement to make, given that you spent most of our engagement in a relationship with someone else. Did you forget about that part? You know, the part where you ended up leaving me for another woman, then tried to beg for my forgiveness way after the fact? And, if that wasn't bad enough —" She paused, clenching her teeth, then locked eyes with John again.

He held out his hand. "Meg, what do you hope to gain from all this?"

She exhaled. "Just the fulfillment of seeing you squirm, even if only for a minute. One would hope you learned your lesson and wouldn't put anyone else through the same misery."

"Meg," he begged.

She glanced over at the young lady, who by now appeared visibly disgusted. "I'd be real cautious about getting in too deep if I were you."

Meg gave John one last glaring stare. "As for you, I'm going to walk out of here and pretend like we never saw each other today. Should you ever run into me on the streets of New York again, pass me by, as if I were a stranger."

With the toss of her hair over her shoulder, once again, Meg was confidently exiting John's presence. This time, she prayed it was for good.

Chapter 14

Parker

"This is crazy, Savannah. Outside of a message to let me know she landed, I haven't heard from Meg once since she's been in New York. I have a terrible feeling about this."

"Parker."

"Seriously. I have that same feeling you get in the pit of your stomach when you know someone is about to break things off with you," he said, standing in the middle of the tile store.

"Park, I'm not trying to undermine your feelings, but there's a chance you may be jumping to conclusions about this one."

"Well, then I guess we'll have to agree to disagree," he replied, scratching his head. "And, by the way. This whole idea of yours, sending me to the tile store to choose samples for the B&B, is not going over very well. There are too many options to choose from. It's enough to drive anybody nuts. I do way better when you bring me a few samples and then we take it from there."

His sister chuckled on the other end of the line. "Sorry, but with a sick kid and husband at home, the likelihood of me getting out today is slim to none. Just pick out a few of our favorite colors, and I'll help you with the rest when I return. As for Meg, I highly doubt she's about to give you a pink slip. She's in New York to focus on her dad and she deserves that time. If you're that worried about where you two stand, maybe it's time for you to step up your game and tell her how you really feel, regardless of the B&B."

"I tried to do a rendition of that when I spoke to her at the airport. It didn't exactly go over so well. Besides, I tell her how I feel all the time. And, outside of this minor incident with me springing the news of the B&B on her, I thought things were going fairly well."

"Parker."

"Yes."

"The one thing I know about you is that you never give up. If something is worth it. If you find any value in it, you're all in. So, this leads me to my next question. Is she worth it to you? Do you see the value in fighting for Meg?" Savannah asked.

He chuckled while inspecting a glass tile on the shelf. "Technically, that was two questions."

"Parker, be serious, please."

He nodded as if she could see him. "She's given me the ability to love again. I thought I completely grew numb after losing Jenna. Now, for the first time, I can actually envision getting married again and asking Meg to be my wife."

Parker found himself gazing at the tile while imagining life prior to meeting Meg. It was lonely and even dark at times. A period in life he'd prefer never to go back to.

The sound of sniffles interrupted his train of thought. "Savannah?"

"Don't mind me. My hormones have been all out of sorts lately. But, more importantly, I'm just so proud of the man you've become. Watching you grow from a boney legged little boy to a man who's been through so much, yet still so resilient. I only wish I could be half as strong as you are."

"You've got to be kidding me, right? You wear your mom, wife, and entrepreneur cape daily, drawing from the strength of a superhero, for goodness' sake."

She laughed. "Thanks, Park. But this conversation is not about me right now; it's about you. The fact that you can see a future with Meg is a huge deal. I'm proud of you."

He reached on the shelf above, choosing a few samples to bring to the front register. "Thanks. Now, if I can just figure out how to convey my love and enthusiasm without scaring her away, then I might be onto something."

"Park, just be yourself and try not to overthink things. I'm sure when she gets back she'll be ready to sit down and have a heart to heart with you. In the meantime, let's pray she's open to helping out with the B&B. We're going to need all hands on deck by the time the baby arrives."

"Tell me about it —" He stopped mid-sentence, realizing what Savannah just uttered. He laid down the tiles, revealing a slow rising smile. "Wait, repeat that again."

"Repeat what?"

"Savannah, stop messing around with me. Repeat what you just said about a baby."

She paused, then burst into laughter. "You mean the part where I said we're having a baby?"

"That's exactly what I thought I heard. That's wonderful news. Congratulations."

"Thank you. And no need to worry. I'll be there to help with the B&B as long as I possibly can," she said.

"I don't know. Once we get into heavy construction, it may not be the best place for you."

"Parker, for now let's just enjoy that we have a sweet bundle of joy on the way. The rest we talk about later."

He handed over his money to the cashier, politely giving her a nod. "Okay, this conversation is not over. I'm not going to be responsible for posing any threats to you having a safe pregnancy."

"I know," she said, dragging her voice.

"Okay, well, in the meantime, I have to get over to the B&B to meet with Barnes. I'm already running late. Wish me luck. You never quite know what to expect when hanging out with him," he teased.

"I'm sure. Call me later and fill me in."

"Will do. Love you, Van. Let the hubs know we'll have to get together when he's feeling better and light up a couple of cigars."

"Ha, I'll tell him. Love you, Park."

* * *

Back at the B&B, Parker knocked on Barnes' door. The place was empty for the remainder of the week, leaving a few days until the next set of guests would arrive.

"Mr. Barnes, it's me, Parker. Just wanted to let you know I'll be downstairs in the living area for our meeting whenever you're ready."

Barnes hollered. "I'll be down in just a minute."

"No rush. Take your time," he replied.

The two had agreed that Barnes would stick around for the rest of the month, showing Parker the ropes. Presumably, Parker would sell his original beach house by then, and Barnes would use the extra time to organize his new living arrangements.

So far, Parker was pleased with how the transaction had

gone between them. Chuck Nesbit had drawn up the contract, making the transition of ownership rather smooth. Now, all that was left was starting the renovations on one house while still conducting business in the other. He would slap on a little paint to brighten up the store, and beef up their booking schedule to ensure steady income.

"Mr. Barnes, good to see you. I hope you didn't rush on my account." Parker smiled.

After a round of vigorous coughing, Barnes replied, "I needed a little nudge. Ever since our last guest left, I've been lazy, napping all day like a bum."

Parker started heading for the kitchen. "Can I get you some water?"

"I need a lot more than water to cure this old rattle in my lungs. Don't worry about me. Have a seat." Barnes waved.

Parker observed as he dropped a large envelope on the coffee table, then shoved it the rest of the way. "Is that additional paperwork pertaining to the B&B?" Parker asked.

"No. According to Chuck, we're all squared away with the B&B. It's officially yours, and I'm forever grateful for the additional time you're giving me to get my business in order," Barnes replied.

"That makes two of us. We're grateful to have you in house, helping us get started with such a big endeavor. I have to tell you, Mr. Barnes, I'm nervous and excited all at the same time. This whole project is really giving me something to look forward to. It's a huge challenge, but we have the best teacher possible, and I really feel like it's going to be successful."

Barnes sat upright in his chair. "I'd like to offer a word of advice, if I may."

"Sure, please do," Parker said.

"Number one. Try to think of the B&B as less of a project and more of a cozy home away from home that you're providing for the guests. Every single person that's ever stayed here raves about the same thing every time. The views of the beach put them in such a relaxed state of mind, they barely want to leave. And then there's the food, which thankfully, the in-house chef will take care of. Between that and the warm and welcoming hospitality, you'll receive five-star reviews every time. So, just remember, it's an experience, and not another one of your projects. It should always be a place where people want to come back to. Get it?"

Parker gazed out the back windows toward the ocean. "Yessir, I hear you loud and clear," he replied, as Meg flashed across his mind. He'd always considered her the perfect person to help add a sense of home to the B&B. The same way she made him feel at home as they spent time together at the beach house.

Barnes nodded. "Yes, that's it. Never forget it. Now, for the real reason I wanted to meet with you today. I'd like for you to open that envelope for me, if you will." He pointed.

As Parker reached for the document, he reminisced about the first time he met Barnes, feeling confident that he would have nothing to do with the B&B. So much had changed since then.

He pulled a piece of paper out with an attorney's letter-head embossed at the top. Puzzled, he looked at Barnes. "Is there something we failed to go over, legally speaking?"

"Not at all. This matter is rather personal, and since I have no one else to call on for help, I was hoping you could —" Barnes paused, turning flush in the face, appearing somewhat choked up.

He pulled it together and continued. "Over the years I've buried loved ones, one by one, probably far more than I'd like to recall. My father was the first to pass. Poor mother was so distraught she could barely take care of herself at the time, let alone make funeral arrangements. Then shortly thereafter, I buried mother. She left two years after my father, to be exact. I guess the old saying is true about folks who end up dying from a broken heart."

After another coughing spell, Barnes continued. "I watched them all live healthy and happy lives back when life was a lot more simple. We used to gather in the living room, listening to old time radio, and when my father saved up enough, we upgraded to watching a television set. Those truly were the good old days, and what made it special was we were all together. But, as I grew older and watched all of them leave this earth, I never considered the day would come where I would be left here all alone. I miss my folks. I miss my wife. And, sadly, no matter how much it hurts that they're gone, there's nothing I can do about it."

A feeling of sadness washed over Parker. "I'm sorry."

"There's no need to be. It's a natural part of life. At least that's what I tell myself every now and again. But, the reason why I called you here is two-fold. That letter is a copy of my last will and testament." He chuckled. "It's not like I have much to leave behind, trust me. But what little I do have, I want my son, Devin Barnes, to have it," Barnes explained.

"How do I fit into the picture?"

Barnes chuckled again. "Well, you're probably going to think I'm nuts for asking you to do this. But, Devin and I haven't seen each other in over twenty, maybe even twenty-five years. He was upset with me when he found out his mother and I were parting ways, naturally so. He blamed me for the entire thing, assuming it was all my fault. Of course, this happened over umpteen years ago. Back when he was barely out of high school."

Parker empathized with him. "Man, that had to be tough."

"It sure was. I was always there for him, still providing and trying to be a strong presence in his life. But the day he realized I was remarrying and joining worlds with Evelyn was a turning point for us. He barely spoke to me much after that. Eventually, he joined the military, cutting off all ties for several years. And, the little contact we've had since then, sadly, hasn't led us to a place of healing," Barnes explained.

"That must be such a heavy burden to carry."

Barnes shook his head. "It was. But I have to make peace with the fact that I've done all I can. It was my intention to leave the B&B to him, but with all the financial trouble I've incurred, there was really no way. What little I have left, I'd like for him to have. And I was wondering if you would mail this to him when the time is right," Barnes said, pointing to the letter. "It's a legal document specifying my wishes, along with a letter. I know I could very well leave the task up to my lawyer, but I was thinking it might feel more personal if done this way. Maybe it would help him to see how much I actually cared."

Parker leaned back. "Mr. Barnes, I'm honored, but—"

"Please? I have the address where he lives. Maybe that, plus a phone call to let him know what to expect — it would mean a great deal."

Parker wondered why everything sounded so final with Barnes. He spoke as if he were counting down the days until he breathed his last breath, as if he knew something and just wasn't telling it.

"Mr. Barnes, I admit to feeling completely inadequate for the job. But, if this is what you want, I'll do everything that I can to help. Especially with the way you stepped out on a limb, making it easy for me to become the next owner of the B&B. It's the least I can do." He paused. "But I can't help but wonder about two things. Is everything okay with your health? And don't you think after all this time your son would want to hear directly from you?"

Barnes stretched out his legs in somewhat of a relaxed position. "Parker, my medical history is longer than a serial killer's rap sheet. I wasn't one of the lucky ones to inherit the family's great health. Instead, I've racked up medical issues and bills piled a mile high. It's part of the reason I had to devise a plan to get rid of this place," he said, waving his hand around. "As for my son, he has no interest in dealing with me. If so, I'd be having this conversation with him right now instead of you."

Parker fought back tears from welling up in his eyes. To lose all your loved ones and to be completely alone while ill was a thought he couldn't bear.

He shoved the contents back into the envelope without reading them. Somehow, he didn't think it was his place. "If you give me his address and telephone number, I'll take care of the rest," Parker said.

"Thank you. Oh, and there's one more thing."

Parker raised a brow. "What's that?"

"The doctor has given me six months to live, maybe eight if I'm lucky. If you could wait until then to make the call —"

Parker offered a final nod, feeling overcome with grief. He'd already been through something similar with Jenna. Therefore, this was hitting home.

Chapter 15

Frankie

Frankie felt the tide rush over her feet as she freely gave in to Christian's caress. It was their third afternoon together, and the very thing she feared was starting to happen.

"Mmm," she moaned. "I can't remember the last time I felt like this," she said.

"How do you feel?" Christian asked.

"Carefree. Feeling the sand in between my toes, and the water taking over my body... it's an amazing feeling."

"But you live out here. One would think you get to experience that feeling any time you want."

As she looked across the sea at the shimmer of light glowing from the setting sun, she couldn't help but disagree. Sure, she lived there, but up until this point, she hadn't really allowed herself to be free.

"There's something to be said about the company you keep. Maybe spending this time together is making all the difference," she said.

Christian's hands slid beside her waist as he delved in for

another kiss. She'd noticed it was something they were becoming good at.

When he came up for air, he said, "These last couple of days with you have been everything I hoped for and more. We may have gotten off to a rocky start, but the end couldn't be sweeter. It kind of makes it difficult to prepare to say goodbye."

A feeling of disappointment washed over Frankie. But she only had herself to blame knowing he wasn't from there. "Shh. Don't talk about leaving just yet. I want to know more about you," she said.

Christian looked down at his wrists, then held his tattoo up for her to see again. "We haven't talked about this yet."

"A.H., that's your sister's initials, right?"

"Right. Anna Halstead," he said, looking off into the distance. "Early last year, I received a phone call from a hospital in San Diego, California. They stated that my sister Anna had been in a head on collision with a man in a four-way intersection. Anna was pronounced dead upon her arrival to the hospital. The man responsible for the accident was arrested and slapped with a DUI."

He grunted. "It always amazes me how a drunk driver gets to walk away without a scratch, while innocent people like Anna —" He paused. "She had her whole life ahead of her. Something about it just doesn't seem fair."

Frankie slipped her hand over his cheek, turning his attention toward her. "It isn't fair. Life isn't fair and you have every right to be angry."

"Oh, you better believe I was angry. At the time of her death, if I had access to him, only God knows what I would've done. Thankfully, I'm no longer in the same state of mind. Anna would've never stood for it, anyway. Any type of outrage was unacceptable to her, knowing the household we grew up in."

"Mmm," Frankie agreed. "That's understandable. But, I also think it's important not to be too hard on ourselves. We all have baggage to unpack. Nobody is perfect."

"True." He snickered.

"What's so funny?"

He glanced her way before picking a large seashell out of the sand. "I told you talking would be therapeutic."

"You sure did."

* * *

Later that evening, Frankie lounged on a chair beside Christian outside the resort. They could practically count the low hanging stars as they cuddled, hoping the night would never end.

"I guess in a short while, you'll be heading upstairs to pack your bags for your morning flight. And, I'll be driving back home," she sighed.

He rubbed his toes next to hers. "How does that make you feel?"

"Sad that our time together is coming to an end. I mean, it was inevitable. We knew this moment would come. But it doesn't make it any easier," she replied.

"Agreed. But, from the start, I've always said that things between us don't have to come to an end," he responded, propping himself up. "The flight to and from Atlanta is just two and a half hours away, making it very possible for us to see each other again."

Frankie closed her eyes. "Let's just enjoy this last hour, savoring every moment, not worrying about what the future may hold."

She could feel him shift. "I guess that's your kind way of telling me you're not interested."

"I didn't say that I'm not interested," she argued.

"Mm hmm."

"I didn't. It's just — long-distance relationships are complicated. It's all fun and good in the beginning when you miss each other so much. But, when the dust settles, you begin to realize just how hard it is. That's when things usually start to fall apart."

"Do you believe in second chances?" he asked.

"Yes, I do. But, third, fourth, and fifth chances — not so much. The odds of finding true love have always been stacked against me. The older I get, the worse it gets. I don't say that to receive sympathy or anything. I just don't have good luck when it comes to love."

Christian looked her in the eyes. "Yet, you desire to have love."

Frankie fixated her attention elsewhere, trying not to reveal her inner thoughts. But boy was he spot on, calling her bluff. She did desire love. But unless it was a perfect fit, in every way, why bother? And, in her book, long distance love didn't come close to being perfect.

"What makes you say a thing like that?" she asked.

"I can feel it. You want to get to know me just as much as I want to get to know you. If only you could let go of those little demons tormenting your mind." He held out his hands. "Look, we're in paradise for goodness' sake. This is a place where dreams are made of, where people fall in love, where people come to escape the ordinary. Frankie, I just want to delve into your sweet lips and escape the ordinary with you. I want to have fun and see where this leads. And, if that means I have to book another flight to return here next month, then I'll do that. Just say you'll have me."

Frankie's pulse throbbed as she tried to maintain her cool.

"Christian, that's the most romantic thing anyone has ever said to me, but are we really being realistic?"

"Hey, I have enough frequent flier miles to come back here every month if you want me to. As for being realistic, all I know is when you meet someone special... someone who makes you feel like you've known them for years, you don't walk away. Not without making a solid effort to see where things go."

She raised up completely, gliding her hand along his. "Christian, you're definitely one of a kind. From the elevator to now, life with you has been nothing but one great adventure." She smiled.

"I'm hoping that's a good thing."

Frankie leaned in, inviting him to delve into her sweet lips as he'd recently offered. When they came up for air, she said, "You're an amazing man. I'd love nothing more than to continue our little adventure, but I need time — just a little time to think things through."

"Sure," Christian responded, cradling her hands in his.

Late that evening, Frankie flopped on her bed and stared at the moonlit window. Yeah, sure, she had to rise early for work in the morning. And, technically, by now, she'd have her lunch packed, her clothes picked out and pressed. But all she could seem to think about was Christian and how quickly he swooped into her life and rocked her world.

Chapter 16

Meg

"Good morning, Dad. How are you feeling today?" Meg asked as she slid a bowl of cinnamon oatmeal before him.

It was a part of her morning routine to get in the kitchen and make breakfast for three, giving Mariam extra time to rest.

"I feel fine, Honey. But I can't help but wonder when you and Mariam are going to allow me to take care of myself again."

"Oh, Dad, it's just a bowl of oatmeal and toast. It's no big deal."

"I know, Sweetheart, and I really appreciate you doing this for me. I do. But how will I ever know if I'm getting stronger if you won't allow me to lift a finger?"

She placed her hand on his shoulder. "When I was sick as a child, did you allow me to do anything?"

"Meg, that was a long time ago. And I did everything for you as a little girl when you were sick because you couldn't do it for yourself. Therein lies the difference. According to the doctor, I am fully capable of moving around this apartment and getting back to the basics, like making my own breakfast."

Meg remained silent as she listened to her dad preach.

"The real question is about you and your state of mind. While you're here in New York taking care of me, what are you avoiding back home?"

As she searched for the right words, a message buzzed through her phone from Frankie. *Thinking about you. I hope all is going well with your dad.*

"Meg? I know you very well. Ever since our conversation in the hospital, you've been in a fog. Have you spoken to your guy friend?" her father asked.

"No. I'm kind of using this time away to clear my mind in hopes that I can start making some level-headed decisions about my future."

"Hmm," he grunted.

She knew her dad's grunt was packed with a ton of wisdom, mixed with a heavy dose of reality, so she chose not to ask.

"By any chance, did you scramble up a few cheese eggs with a side of bacon?" he asked.

"Dad! That's exactly what landed you in the hospital in the first place."

She turned around to the familiar sight of his belly jiggling. "You're so bad."

"A man can dream, can't he?"

Meg nodded. "I guess."

She returned to the kitchen just a few steps away to cover Mariam's breakfast, then briefly replied to Frankie's message. "All is well with dad. We're home now and he's back to his usual shenanigans."

From the dining area, her dad yelled, "Speaking of dreams, Meg. Wouldn't you say the time is long overdue for you to start pursuing them?"

"That's exactly what I did when I left here, remember? It's not my fault the initial plan backfired on me."

As Meg reached for the dirty pot to scrub, she flashed back to her run-in with John. Of all the grocery stores in Manhattan, did they really have to choose the same one? It had been such an honor to forget his existence, and such a disappointment to be reminded of him again.

Her father snuck up on the right side of her. "This is supposed to be the most exciting time of your life, figuring out what direction you're heading in next, and pursuing your dreams. You should be enthusiastic instead of downtrodden. Yeah, sure, so you had a minor setback with the first job. But you don't have a track record of quitting and you can easily take your experience elsewhere."

Meg squirted the dish detergent on the sponge and proceeded to scrub. "I know, Dad. I guess I just needed a chance to hit the reset button and recalibrate, if you will. Haven't you ever been through something that just feels like a setback?"

"Ha. Have I? Right now, if I didn't go through this little health scare of mine, I was supposed to be working on a new case at work. This, in my opinion, is the perfect example of a setback. Then there's the fact that I'm in my seventies and still can't retire — not that I really want to, but it's always nice to know you have the option."

"What do you mean, you can't retire? The other day, you said you weren't ready to," she said.

Her dad shook his head. "I'm not ready to, Sweetheart. But, even if I were, have you noticed the cost of living in New York these days? The prices are going through the roof. Plus, back when things were getting a little tight for Mariam and I, we made the decision to borrow from our retirement. Not the end of the world, of course, but we'll have to make adjustments. Yet again, another setback."

"But, Dad."

"No buts, love. Life is what you make it. Trust me, there's not one decision that Mariam and I haven't consciously made and planned together. We will be just fine. But, it's about time you learned this lesson while you are still young. Life will be filled with constant setbacks. It's what you choose to do with the setbacks that matters most."

Meg turned off the faucet while watching her father reach in the fridge. "You're right, Dad. You're totally right."

"I hope I wasn't too harsh, Honey," he said.

"No. Not at all. Sometimes I need a good kick in the pants every now and again."

"Good. In that case, I have one more kick in the pants for you." He smiled.

"Oh goodness."

"You can handle this because you know it's coming from a place of love. Tonight, I want us to sit down and search for a flight back to the island," he said, placing his hand across his chest. "Clearly, I'm going to be fine, but you, on the other hand, need time to get your plans in order."

Meg stood firm. "But I just got here."

"I know, and we'll make the best of this time, I promise. We'll even make plans for Mariam and I to come and visit when the doctor gives me the okay. But, in the meantime, there's an opportunity waiting on the island for you. And, from the sound of things, there's a special man waiting on pins and needles to hear if you'll accept."

Meg closed her eyes, resting in the comforting words of reassurance from her dad. Accomplishing her mission of laying eyes on him gave her the assurance she needed. But he was right. There was a man waiting to hear from her back on the island. A man she'd hoped hadn't given up on her.

* * *

"Casey, your place looks absolutely amazing," Meg said, as her eyes wandered from one end of the living room to the other. "If I didn't know any better, I'd think you hired an interior decorator."

"Well, I'm glad you know better. There's no way Craig would ever see the logic in such an expense. You know how he is — I can hear him now. *Oh, just buy a new plant and throw a new picture on the wall. That oughta do the trick.*" She laughed.

"I know. But, clearly he trusts your sense of style. Plus, Craig is so good to you. That's what matters most, right?"

Casey agreed. "There's no denying that part. I count my blessings every day. Speaking of the apartment, thank you for being flexible and bypassing the idea of going to a restaurant today. I wore myself out waiting in line at the DMV this morning, so I thought, why not enjoy a little time with just the two of us before the kids get home from school?"

Meg gazed twenty floors down, admiring the city views. "This plan was perfect," she said, while people watching. "I can only imagine the beautiful views you'll have during this upcoming holiday season. With the street lamps being decorated, and hustling and bustling in their winter gear. And, let's not forget about stopping by the hot pretzel stand. There's something about living in the city that's just so magical," she said.

"Wait a minute — please don't tell me you're ready to move back."

"No," Meg replied, turning to embrace Casey's belly. "Although I'd give anything to live closer to you and the kids again. Especially now that you have another sweet bundle of joy on the way. Life just isn't the same without having all of you near."

Casey patted the cushion on the couch. "Are you feeling a little homesick?"

"Maybe that's part of it. But, I think the biggest ordeal has been finding my sense of belonging. I'm trying everything I possibly can. I joined a new book club, was thinking about signing up for an exercise class, but haven't quite gotten around to it yet."

Casey interrupted. "Um, let's not forget you found a new man," she said, snapping her fingers.

Meg nodded with a lazy smile. "You're right. We can't forget about Parker. But he'll likely forget about me if I don't get my act together soon. I'll have to save that story for later. Then there's my job — or shall I say the job I used to have, but I quit... again another story for later. No matter which way you slice it, everything is not going as smoothly as I originally planned."

Casey flopped both hands down on her lap. "Oh wow, that's a lot, and I can see how you might feel overwhelmed. But, let's not forget how much you had to overcome before moving to the island. I won't go as far as saying his name, reminding you of the past — but I will say, I think you're allowed to take some additional time to figure your life out."

Meg flipped her hair back, reliving the scene in her mind. "Trust me, running into John and his girlfriend at the grocery store was all the reminder I needed."

"Nooo."

"Yessss." Meg laughed to keep from crying. "I'm so over him, Case. I really am. But, the nerve — the gall he had to come up to me as if everything is good between us." She sighed. "His level of arrogance never ceases to amaze me."

"I'll bet. Did you haul off and slap him one good time simply for being a jerk?" Casey asked.

"Does that sound like something I'd ever do?" Meg teased.

"Aren't you the same woman who doused the man in water right before calling off the wedding?"

Meg squinted. "That was just a minor physical infraction

on my part. This time he got away with a warning never to speak to me again."

"Ooh, do tell," Casey replied.

She nestled into the couch, letting out a long breath through her nose. "I wish I had something new to tell, but you know how the story goes, Case. Once a liar and a cheat, always a liar and a cheat. I'm just disappointed that I walked around blindly for three years, wasting my own precious time."

Casey protested. "Sorry, but I beg to differ. You didn't waste your time, Meg. Instead, you learned a lot of valuable lessons, you grew stronger, and you stood up for yourself when the time was right. And, in the end, you managed to escape the toxic web he weaved, moved to paradise, and fell in love with the most wonderful man you've ever known."

Meg bounced upright. "I like the sound of that. It's all been somewhat of a tropical escape, if you will. An escape that allowed me to end a very bad chapter and start all over again. Now that you put it that way, it sounds so —"

Casey interrupted. "Romantic? Invigorating?"

Again, Meg slouched back, this time immersed in a heavy dose of guilt. "I've been such a selfish brat as of late. I've been so caught up in my own drama that I barely took the time to hear Parker out. The way I stormed out of the party and brushed him off on the phone," she said.

Casey supported her back as she rose out of a nearby chair. "Talk to me, Meg. You sound like you have a lot on your mind."

When her friend joined her on the same couch, the flood-gate of emotions she'd been holding onto finally came pouring out.

"Case, where do I begin? Have you ever been at a point in your life where you have absolutely no idea what's coming next?" she asked.

"Yeah, I'm sure we all have."

Meg nodded. "Well, until now, that's exactly where I've been. Turns out the man of my dreams is so good to me. Instead of me appreciating it, I nearly ran away from him. Oh, and then there's my so-called glamorous dream job, which I actually ended up quitting right before coming here to New York."

"Say what?"

"You heard me right. All this in the midst of dad having a health scare. Even though, funny thing with that is, he feels strong, and is already trying to send me back home."

The two chuckled.

"That sounds like your dad," Casey replied.

"It does, doesn't it? Although I know what Daddy is up to. He means well and just wants to see me get back to the island so I can focus on my dreams."

Meg felt Casey's warm hand patting her on the shoulder as she began to speak. "Why don't you listen to your father, Meg? So, things haven't gone exactly the way you thought they would with the job. Big deal. You'll find a new job in no time. But first things first. Get back there and go after your man. Let him know how much you've missed him and squash whatever nonsense that caused you to walk out in the first place."

She giggled. "Just like that, huh? And what if he's not willing to hear what I have to say?"

"Oh, please. Do you really think he'll be able to resist that sweet smile?" Casey asked.

"Thank you, Case. You always have a way of lifting me up when I'm feeling at my lowest."

"No problem. That's what I'm here for. Although, I do have to ask, why did you run out on the guy again?"

"Oh boy, you're really going to have a field day with this, but here's the short and sweet version. He just bought a new business. A B&B to be precise. And, he publicly presented myself and his sister to come work with him before this huge crowd at his house party. He didn't really do anything wrong, it was just a lot for me to digest. I know it sounds stupid but, ultimately I felt pressured, I panicked, and then I left."

Meg watched as Casey's eyebrows folded together. "Go ahead and say it."

"Oh no, not me. I don't have a word to say. But I'm sure you know what I'm thinking," Casey replied, then got up, making herself busy in the kitchen. "Want something to drink?"

Meg followed. "No, what I want is your honest opinion. You think I overreacted, don't you?"

"Well."

"Come on Case. If there is one thing you and my dad have in common, it's your transparency. I can see it written all over your face. And, I should go on record and say, in my defense, the man was planning on looking for his next house to renovate and that's it. I knew nothing about the purchase of this B&B, and from what I know, it still sounds like a decision he made on a whim."

Casey chugged back a tall glass of water, then laid it down. "Is he a good businessman? As in, he usually has a history of making good decisions?"

"Yeah."

"Is he trustworthy? Dependable? And all the other things a woman usually looks for in a man?" she asked.

Meg nodded her head. "Yes."

"Final question. Is he the complete opposite of that low-life who goes by the name of —"

Meg raised her hand. "Alright, I see where you're going with this."

"Good. In that case, go hear the man out. And stop getting in your own way. Agreed?"

Meg lifted her arms, delving in for the biggest hug. "Agreed. Now, enough about me and my drama. Bring me up to date on the pregnancy. I want to hear all about it."

Chapter 17

Frankie

Boarding flight *two-thirty-seven to Hartsfield Jackson International,* the attendant announced. Frankie locked eyes with Christian, more exchanging soft smiles. Trying hard to hold on to her nerves, she handed over her ticket, then proceeded forward.

At their seats, she scooted over to the window seat, while Christian took the middle.

"So, we're really doing this?" Frankie asked.

"We made it this far. Of course, they haven't closed the door yet, so technically I guess you have time to —"

She interrupted, placing her finger over his mouth. "Christian, the moment you showed up at my door, I knew I was ready to pack my bags and take this adventure back to Atlanta with you. There's something between us. Something I'm not ready to give up so easily without exploring."

"I'm glad to hear it, but I have to say, you really caught me by surprise. I had plans of pulling out all the tricks, even getting on my knees and begging you if I had to. I never expected you to say yes, but I still was going to try. I guess you're every bit of an adventurous woman, just like you described."

She felt his breath as he leaned in, pressing his warm lips over hers. Repeatedly, Frankie received the taste of his lips until the flight attendant broke their symphony.

"Excuse me, I hate to interrupt the lovebirds, but sir, your seatbelt needs to be fastened."

Frankie's body lunged upward, grasping the sheets. With her t-shirt covered in warm perspiration, she realized her mind had been totally consumed by a dream. She wasn't on board a flight with Christian and he wasn't kissing her lips. It was just another ordinary weekend, and she was all alone.

The phone rang, but the temptation to lie back down and ignore it was too great. She'd rather stare at the ceiling, drowning in her own misery, than be social at the moment. It was just her luck that she'd actually meet a guy, fall for him, and then watch as he walked right out of her life, returning to the place he called home. She'd grown used to it by now. It was just the way things always seemed to work out.

After two minutes of quiet, the phone rang again. Fighting the urge to bury herself under a pillow, Frankie lifted the phone. "Hello?"

"Frankie?" Meg said.

Trying not to sound disappointed, she replied, "Hey, Meg."

"You sound like you've been run over by a Mack truck. Did I wake you?"

Frankie rose, sliding to the edge of the bed, in search of her slippers. "No, just lying here allowing time to pass. How's everything going with your dad?"

"It's going well, but definitely a unique visit for sure. He's actually giving me orders to pack my bags and head back home — today," Meg said.

"So soon? Gee, what's the big rush? You just got there."

"I know. We were originally planning for the end of the weekend, but we were able to find a last-minute deal on the flight. He says he's feeling pretty strong and being the wonderful dad that he is, I think he's trying to give me the push I need to head back home and get my life in order."

Frankie shuffled to her dresser drawer. "Ahh, your father is a good man. I would imagine one of the first things on your list of to do's would be to see Parker."

"Yes, not only seeing him, but having a very much needed heart-to-heart."

Frankie continued rummaging through the drawer, pulling out her most recent bathing suit purchase. She held it up, admiring the floral petal design. They may have been entering the winter season shortly, but with temps in the eighties, it would be therapeutic to walk along the shore and maybe even go for a swim. "I'm sure a heart-to-heart will be like wonderful medicine for the soul."

"Hmm, I guess I never thought of it that way. But, if it's good for the soul, then God knows I'll take it. In the meantime, my flight lands this evening around six. I was hoping you could do me a favor," Meg asked.

Frankie stood before a mirror. "Do you need someone to pick you up at the airport?"

"Pretty please."

"No problem. I'll be there with time to spare."

"Thank you," Meg replied.

"You bet. Text me the information and be safe."

After concluding the call, Frankie felt helplessly numb. She was going through the motions, doing and saying all the right things. But, deep down, what she wondered most was when the feeling of missing Christian would finally go away.

On Monday morning, she'd need to get back into the swing of things, carrying on with life as usual, instead of rehearsing over and over her last interaction with him.

Her phone rang again. This time, with a playful eye-roll she answered on the first ring. "What did you forget now?"

Meg's voice piped up. "Frankie, I just checked the weather, and it looks like the island had terrible storms last night. I just wanted to call back and make sure everything was okay at the house."

Frankie paused, considering everything that happened after parting ways with Christian, but she had no recollection of a storm. "Sorry, hate to break it to ya, but you know how sound I sleep at night. A tornado could've blown through here and I wouldn't know a darn thing about it."

Meg chuckled. "You're right. I forgot who I was talking to. In that case, go on and get back to your day."

"Okay."

"Oh — and, Frankie, one more thing."

Frankie froze, fearing her roommate could discern the sound of disappointment in her voice. "Yeah?"

"You and I have some catching up to do. Not everything is about me and Parker. I want to hear about what's going on with you."

Feeling relieved, Frankie said, "Don't worry, there'll be plenty of time for that. For now, you just focus on getting back safely."

* * *

Of all the absentminded things to do, Frankie left the house with her mind in a fog, leaving behind her cellphone and wallet. At this point, she didn't even care. Did she really need to be joined to the hip with an electronic device? Prior to the invention, she'd spent decades without it. And did she really need to stop by Terry's Food Stand to spill her heart out to Terry over delicious comfort food? Okay, probably yes to the latter, but at this point she'd have to do without both.

So, instead, she found a bench not far from the food stand, allowing her to overlook the tranquil water.

In the middle of a mindless gaze, a man's voice resounded. "Would you like some company?"

She turned slightly, not feeling the least bit amused. "Thanks, but no thank you. I don't mean to be rude but —"

The man held his hand up. "It's okay, I get it. You have a good day, ma'am."

"Mm," she grunted.

As Frankie returned her gaze to people and wave watching, she contemplated her current state of mind. *You are a strong woman who will not allow one small little setback to ruin your mood for the week.*

Again, her thought pattern was interrupted by a male voice. "I guess if the other guy didn't get an invitation to sit, then I really don't stand a chance."

With a quick turn at the recognition of his voice, she said, "Christian."

He held out his arms, pretending to self inspect. "I think it's me, in the flesh. The real question is, what are you doing out here by yourself without answering your cellphone?"

A slow smile smeared across Frankie's face, lighting her up from the inside out. "No, the real question is, what are you doing here?"

As he crept closer, he began to explain. "An angel saw to it that my boss would give me a new assignment, reviewing another resort right here on the island."

Frankie reared back, seemingly confused. "But why would

they allow you to fly all the way back to Atlanta, only to turn around again?"

Christian slid his hand over hers as he took a seat on the bench. "Ha, that's a good question. You're assuming that corporate makes decisions based on logic. Every now and again, they're known for their blunders. This, my dear, would be one of them."

She slid closer. "Wow, I certainly didn't see this coming."

"Neither did I. As a matter of fact, I just got back within the hour. I haven't even checked in at the other hotel yet."

Frankie shook her head in disbelief and chuckled. "Yet somehow you managed to magically find your way to me?"

"You left me no choice but to come looking for you. When you didn't answer your phone, I had to make sure you were okay."

"Well, I'm fine," she said.

"Are you? You didn't seem so happy just a minute ago."

Again, she smiled. "How long were you standing there again?"

"Not long. I could just tell by your tone that something was off. You dismissed that poor guy so quickly he didn't stand a chance," he said, brushing her hair out of the way. "But when you saw me, I was hoping you'd tell me how much you missed me," he explained, allowing his finger to trace down the side of her cheek. "I was hoping you'd tell me how happy you are to see me, and —"

"And? There's more? Man, you had your hopes up high," she teased.

"I guess I did, because I was also hoping you'd tell me that we belong together, and there's no way you could possibly allow me to leave this island again without the two of us being an item."

Frankie's heart began thumping so out of control she feared he could hear it.

"Christian," she whispered, turning her head away.

"I couldn't stop thinking about you, Frankie. I wanted to call you before taking off for Atlanta, but I held back, trying to respect your space. I thought about you the entire flight there, and then again the whole way back. I'm not quite sure what you've done to me, but I can't get you out of my mind."

Frankie noticed the internal battle she'd been fighting had dissipated. As a matter of fact, everything felt good in her life, now that Christian was back again. "How long are you here for this time?"

"Two weeks," he replied.

"Christian, somehow I get this funny feeling you had a lot to do with getting this next assignment."

He laughed. "Maybe I had a little something to do with it," he said, pinching his fingers together. "But either way, it was all worth it. Another couple of weeks in paradise with the woman I —"

Frankie raised an eyebrow. "What was that?"

"What?" he asked, looking around.

"What were you about to say? With the woman I —"

Without hesitation, Christian answered. "Love. With the woman I love. It may sound kind of premature, but I know myself well enough to know that you've captured my heart, Frankie. I'd book another round-trip flight to be with you any time. You're worth it."

On the inside, Frankie was screaming uncontrollably. But, externally, she was as calm as a cucumber as she slid the palm of her hands over his face. "Christian, I was heartbroken when you left. Now that you're back, all I want to do is relive the kiss from our last night again, and again, and again."

"There doesn't have to be anymore last nights, Frankie," he said.

"Prove it to me. Kiss me, Christian."

From that moment on, things became very clear to Frankie. The only plans she would be making was to message Parker, asking him to pick up Meg while she became reacquainted with love.

Chapter 18

Meg

O n the flight back, Meg vacillated between gazing at the clouds and rehearsing what she would say when she saw Parker. In between thoughts, she occasionally took a break to flip through the chapters of her new book. That's when it hit her. The last time she attended the book club there was a woman who asked, *"What kind of advice would you give to a character like Shelby? How does one see their way out of a continuous spiral of wrong decision-making, just to fill an empty void?"*

Thoughts of the run-in with John flashed in Meg's mind; even thoughts of Iris came to the forefront. Although, if Meg were being honest, quitting her job at the resort wasn't a wrong decision; it was just an unexpected one.

Meg spoke out loud. "I'd tell her it's time to start facing her truth," she said, causing the passenger to her left to flash a look.

After a brief smile, Meg returned to the pages of her book. In her opinion, Shelby, the character, wouldn't likely change until she was ready to be honest with herself. She'd probably wake up one day with an overwhelming sense that something had to give. Whether it be a sign that it was time for healing, or perhaps a dumb act committed by the cheating husband, causing her to nearly slap him in the middle of aisle five. Either way, the trigger for change would surely come, and when it did, she'd act on it.

For Meg, her trigger for change had arrived, and in just a few short hours, she planned to take action.

In the meantime, she'd finish the remaining pages of her book, longing to see what happened in the end.

* * *

To describe the remainder of the flight as a nerve-wracking event would be an understatement. The pilot had circled for almost an hour, waiting for the right moment to land. Now that she was finally on the ground, all Meg wanted was to grab her overhead bags and head home.

Meg threw her duffle bag over her shoulder, feeling thankful for wearing her flip-flops and jeans. The hike past the luggage area to the exit would be a lot more pleasant as a result.

With a press of a button, she dialed her dad's house.

"Hello?" Mariam answered.

"Hi, Mariam, it's Meg. Just wanted to let you know I made it safe."

"Oh, dear. I'm glad to hear it. Your father and I were starting to worry."

Meg peered around the airport, noticing outside the rain was coming down in buckets. "Yeah, apparently the Bahamas is being hit with storms. That mixed with the occasional lightning strike is enough to throw a flight off schedule."

Meg could hear her dad joining the line.

He spoke up. "Sweetheart, is that you?"

"Yes, it's me. No need to worry. I'm here safe, and I'm sure

Frankie will pull up at any moment now. I'm sure the storm caused delays traveling to the airport."

"Okay, well, I just wanted to get on here and let you know how much I miss you. I hope you know that me encouraging you to return home had everything to do with us wanting the best for your future, Honey. As soon as you get your new job in order, we'll make it our business to fly out and visit with you," he said.

"I know, Dad. Honestly, that's what I've always loved about you. You know exactly when I need a kick in the pants and you aren't afraid to give it." She smiled.

As Meg looked up, her mouth slipped wide open. In the distance, she saw the most handsome version of Parker Wilson she'd ever seen. He presumably was searching for her but hadn't locked eyes yet.

"Hey, Dad. I'll be holding you to it. As soon as I land my new job and you're healthy enough to travel, I want you and Mariam to come out and spend some time," she said.

"You bet, Honey."

As she continued, Parker was heading in another direction. "Hey guys, it looks like my ride is here. I'll be in touch soon, okay?"

"Sounds good, Sweetheart. Oh, one more thing," her dad said.

"Yes?"

"Go get him, tiger." Meg paused, smiling uncontrollably as she knew just what her dad was referring to.

"Thanks, Dad."

Once the line was disconnected, Meg began to yell, "Parker... Parker."

When he stopped and turned around, Meg's heart nearly stopped along with him. She'd almost forgotten how he had a way of doing that to her.

"Meg," he said.

In slow motion, she took steps closer to him, noticing his soaked shirt and wet hair. In her eyes, the wet look was completely irresistible. "What are you doing here?" She smiled.

Meg's smile was met with an all-consuming kiss, one that nearly made her feel lightheaded.

When Parker came up for air, he said, "I need you, Meg. Nothing else in this life matters to me if I don't have you in it."

As she inhaled the scent of his laundry detergent, she exhaled the words, "I need you, too."

"You do?" he asked.

"Yes, Parker. I really do. When I left here, I was burdened with so much uncertainty. I don't know. It just seemed like I was starting to question everything." She hung her head low. "Including the decision I made to move out here."

Parker removed the duffle bag from her arm. "Wow. I knew things weren't sounding good between us, but I didn't realize it was that bad."

Meg replied, "It wasn't you. It was me being unsure of myself. The biggest lesson I've learned — when you make a major change in your life, you can't guarantee it won't come with setbacks."

Parker kissed her softly on the forehead. "I can handle an occasional setback every now and then. What I can't handle is ever losing you."

Meg pretended to dust off his shirt. "If you keep looking this good you won't have to worry about losing anybody," she teased.

Parker looked down at his clothes. "Yeah, the sky let loose just as soon as I walked out of the parking deck. But, hey I don't care. I'd get soaked for you any day of the week."

"Aww, that's sweet, babe. What do you say we get out of

here? I want to hear all about how you ended up being the one to come pick me up. Plus, we have a lot of catching up to do."

Parker grabbed her hand and began tugging her along. "Follow me. I know this cozy beach house where we can have something to eat and talk. We can consider it our last little rendezvous."

Meg paused. "Why?"

"Because by tomorrow, by this time, the house will be sold."

This time Meg planted a kiss. "I'm so proud of you," she whispered.

"Thank you. Oh, and before I forget. I think Frankie may be occupied for a little while at the house. But she did give me strict orders to pick you up and have you home by later on tonight."

Meg looked at him with a curious smile as they left the airport. Walking hand-in-hand, they were practically oblivious to the rainfall.

* * *

Meg grasped her chest as she listened to Parker bringing her up to speed. "Oh my. What a sad story, Parker. If Old Man Barnes is terminally ill, don't you think his son would want to know before he dies?"

Parker nodded. "One would think. Barnes couldn't even bring himself to verbally tell me. I had to read about his diagnosis on a piece of paper. As sad as it is, it's not up to me to push Barnes to do anything he doesn't want to do. The last thing I'd ever want to do is break his trust."

Meg agreed. "I understand. It's just heartbreaking, that's all."

"Yeah, well, just remember when the two of you meet, don't say a word about it. I put all his documents away in a safe.

For now, it's back to business as usual, unless he says otherwise."

Meg rested across the couch, taking in the evening breeze. The rain had finally let up, revealing a beautiful, tropical sky. "So, you still want me to meet Barnes?" she asked.

"Of course I do. But, just so you know, I don't have any crazy ideas in mind. I'm fully prepared to hire a manager should you decide the job is not for you," he explained.

"Parker, I guess what I really need to understand is, how would all this work? There are so many questions running through my mind. Like, what if we bump heads and stop getting along — would you expect me to quit and find another job? And, how certain are you about keeping this business afloat? This is a new venture for all of us, you know."

Parker slid onto the couch beside her, kneading his hands over her shoulder blades. "The way I envision this thing going is, we'd be making plans that stretch far beyond us, just working together at the B&B. Nowhere in my plans do I see a future without you, Meg. As for your second question, I think our business model is pretty solid. We have the best of both worlds, including Barnes and his good friends who also own a B&B to provide support. We really can't go wrong. Of course, the offer only stands if you can really see yourself managing a B&B. If not, it won't impact a thing with us."

The feeling of his hands kneading into her shoulders was nearly enough to make her lose focus.

"I want the same future that you speak of, and if that future begins at the B&B, then I'm all in," she responded.

"Really?"

Meg rose, adjusting herself in front of him. "Really. And, since we're being completely candid, there's something else I should tell you."

"Oh no. I can tell from the sound of your voice, this isn't good," he said.

She felt a nervous twitch in her stomach, but bravely proceeded. "I saw my ex when I was in New York."

Suddenly, the mood shifted. She contemplated whether it was necessary to say anything at all. But Meg had rehearsed it on the plane and knew it was an important part of keeping an honest relationship.

"And," Parker replied.

"And — I would've gladly passed him by, not speaking at all if he hadn't gone out of his way to get my attention."

"That must've been awkward," he said.

She shook her head. "Awkward for him, maybe. But, for me, the whole experience was a reminder of how much of a good thing I have here at home — with you."

"Did you really need to see him to figure that out?"

Meg felt moisture welling up in her eyes. She hated creating even an ounce of doubt in his mind.

She sniffled. "It wasn't just seeing him, Parker. Running into John was the last thing I expected. It was the whole experience. I needed to leave the island for a few days, see my dad, and clear my mind. I've been through way too many changes as of late. I owed it to myself to take time out and make sure I'm on the right track."

"Mm," he grunted.

"It may not be what you wanted to hear, but it's the truth. All I can say is I'm ready to move forward now, and I'm hoping I can do so with you."

Meg could hear several loud heartbeats through her eardrum before he tugged her by the hands, pulling her closer.

Parker patted his lap. "I understand."

"You do?"

"Yes. Take a moment and look around you. Do you recognize this place?" he asked.

Meg giggled. "It's your beach house, silly. Soon to be sold beach house, but you get the idea."

"Right. But, it's so much more. This is the same house where we first met, and later became the house where I shared my world with you. Meg, my world was broken before we met. And it took way more than a little trip to New York for me to figure my life out and get things right. So, what I'm trying to tell you is, from the bottom of my heart, I understand. If you need more time or if ever you need someone to talk to, I understand."

Her heart melted into what felt like a thousand pieces. All she ever really wanted was a strong, trustworthy man with a kind and gentle heart. So far, Parker had proven that he was more than qualified.

"Thank you," she said, shedding a tear. But she didn't cry long. Instead, she leaned in closer to his body, losing herself in a kiss.

* * *

Meg pushed open the door of Sabrina's bookstore with Frankie trailing behind. She turned and whispered, "You are going to absolutely love these women. The book of the month is awesome, but I swear, there's something totally therapeutic about sitting in on the discussions."

Frankie rolled her eyes. "We'll see, Meg. The time I needed therapy most was when I was on the dating scene. Now that I'm taken, and no longer on the market, I actually feel like I have my sanity back." Frankie chuckled.

Meg stopped at the display table, picking up a book for Frankie. "You've got it all wrong, Frankie. Us women need circles like this. It's uplifting and, as you would say, good for the soul."

"But, a book club, Meg. Really? This is not real therapy."

"It's even better. It's a sisterhood, a group, people you can discuss real-life issues with and be yourself around," Meg replied.

"But this is only your second visit with the club. You mean to tell me you walked away feeling like that after only attending one time?"

Meg laughed. "Yes, trust me on this. I know a good fit when I see one," she replied, tapping the book. "The issues are real and the group is a good fit. If you walk away tonight, feeling like it was a waste of your time, I promise you never have to come again. Agreed?"

Frankie reached for her wallet. "Okay."

After paying for the book, they joined the group, listening as the same leader began. "So, ladies, what do you think? It looks as if Shelby has given her cheating husband an ultimatum. Either he gets his act together and commits to couples therapy, or he has to be out by the end of the month. Any thoughts?"

A reader called out. "Clearly, she's not ready to let go. Who knows, maybe the relationship can be salvaged if he's finally willing to do the right thing."

Another woman raised her hand. "The problem I have with this whole scenario is trust. Once the trust is broken, and in this case not once but multiple times, I'm sorry, but I'm done."

Frankie nodded, then nudged Meg. "She's got that right," she whispered.

The leader of the book club directed her attention toward Frankie. "Do you have something you'd like to add?"

Meg pointed forward toward the speaker. "She's talking to you. Speak up."

"Oh. Um, I was just agreeing with the last comment, that's all," Frankie said.

The leader continued. "Would you kick him to the curb or go to couples therapy?"

Meg watched as Frankie nervously fumbled. "If I may speak on behalf of my friend —" she said. "I'd like to think we'd all respond on a case-by-case basis. Wouldn't you agree? I mean, think about it. We all have various thresholds. Women surprise themselves every day as they discover just how much they can endure. But, until Shelby is ready to face her fears or make a final decision one way or the other, she's going to continue extending their time together. Don't be fooled by an ultimatum. It doesn't mean she's done with him."

Meg felt Frankie tap her on the arm. She watched as her friend gained the confidence to speak up. "But there also comes a time when we've finally had enough. By then, it's a wrap. There are no more ultimatums, no more talks, no more extended goodbyes. We just want out. Period. I personally would rather invest my time elsewhere. Some women would stay and forgive. It's like Meg said, everybody has a different threshold."

Meg felt a big smile emerging. "That's it. The key is Shelby has to find her own way out, her own escape to happiness. It has to come from within herself, whether he's on board or not."

The leader agreed. "Yes, and that's not to say people can't make each other happy in a relationship, but if you're waiting around, depending on your mate to be your sole source of happiness, then you're in trouble."

Another reader commented. "I still say she should kick his butt out, but that's just my two cents." That comment, of course, created a roar of laughter among the others.

* * *

The following morning Meg attended the closing with Parker, then took a ride over to the B&B to meet Barnes. As he pulled up, she saw the sign that read Bed and Breakfast. "So, I guess this is a pretty big day. The beach house is officially sold, and by this evening you'll be moving into the B&B with Barnes."

Parker smiled. "Sounds crazy, doesn't it?"

"No, not really. I think it was nice of you to let him stay a while longer. It's been his home for so long. I can only imagine the memories this place must hold. Especially memories of his wife."

She watched as Parker fiddled with the steering wheel. "Speaking of his wife, I didn't mention it earlier, but it turns out she used to serve at a food bank with my wife Jenna before she got sick."

Meg gasped. "Whoa, what are the odds?"

"I know. Tell me about it."

"Do you think that's why you and Barnes were able to hit it off so well?"

He stared forward. "It crossed my mind in the beginning, but now, the real reason he reached out to me is clear as day. Yes, he did his research and learned that I could turn this place around, and yes, financially, he was underwater. But, most importantly, I think he sees something in me that reminds him of his son. Or at a minimum, the relationship he desires to have with his son."

Meg's eyes scanned across the entrance of the B&B to the gift shop and beyond. "Well, in that case, I'm glad the two of you were able to cross paths. I'm also glad we still have him on board to help us with this undertaking. Two B&B's, a gift shop, and not a staff member in sight. Should I be worried?"

Parker slid his hand over hers. "We have an amazing chef, part-time help when the gift shop reopens, Savannah, who's a wonderful designer, you as our amazing manager, and we have —"

The two leaned across the center console, gazing into each other's eyes. Simultaneously, they said, "and we have each other."

The End.

Ready to read book 3, Tropical Moonlight? Click here for more details.

New Tropical Breeze Series!

Can she find love when she's healing from heartache?

After a painful end to a long engagement, all Meg wants out of life is a fresh start.

She can't think of a better way to begin than by advancing her career in the hotel industry. When an opportunity comes along to accept a position at a five-star resort, she secures a beach house, packs her bags, and heads to the Bahamas.

But her oasis has been sold in an auction and the new owner and heartthrob, Parker Wilson, has no intention of holding onto a contract.

She'll have nowhere to stay, nowhere to heal, nowhere to grow if she gives in to his flippant attitude about her future.

When Meg digs her heels in and refuses to leave, will this drive them further into the arena of enemies? Or will they find common ground and potentially become lovers?

Tropical Encounter is a clean beach read with a splash of romance that's sure to give you all the feels.

Pull up your favorite beach chair and watch as Meg and Parker's story unfolds!

Tropical Breeze Series:
>   *Tropical Encounter: Book 1*
>   *Tropical Escape: Book 2*
>   *Tropical Moonlight: Book 3*
>   *Tropical Summers: Book 4*
>   *Tropical Brides: Book 5*

Solomons Island Series

She's single, out of a job, and has a week to decide what to do with her life.

He lost his fiancé to a fatal accident while serving in the coast guard.

Will a chance encounter lead Clara and Mike to find love?

Clara's boss, Joan Russell, was a wealthy owner of a beachfront mansion, who recently passed away. Joan's estranged family members have stepped in, eager to collect their inheritance and dismiss Clara of her duties.

With the clock winding down, will Clara find a job and make a new life for herself on Solomons Island? Will a chance encounter with Mike lead her to meet the man of her dreams? Or will Clara have to do the unthinkable and return home to a family who barely cares for her existence?

This women's divorce fiction book will definitely leave you wanting more! If you love women's fiction and clean romance, this series is for you. Embark on a journey of new beginnings and pick up your copy today!

Solomons Island Series:

Beachfront Inheritance: Book 1

Beachfront Promises: Book 2

Beachfront Embrace: Book 3

Beachfront Christmas: Book 4

Beachfront Memories: Book 5

Beachfront Secrets: Book 6

Pelican Beach Series

She's recently divorced. He's a widower. Will a chance encounter lead to true love?

If you like sweet romance about second chances then you'll love The Inn At Pelican Beach!

At the Inn, life is filled with the unexpected. Payton is left to pick up the pieces after her divorce is finalized. Seeking a fresh start, she returns to her home town in Pelican Beach.

Determined to move on with her life, she finds herself

caught up in the family business at The Inn. It may not be her passion, but anything is better than what her broken marriage had to offer. Payton doesn't wallow in her sorrows long before her opportunity at a second chance shows up. Is there room in her heart to love again? She'll soon find out!

In this first book of the Pelican Beach series, passion, renewed strength, and even a little sibling rivalry are just a few of the emotions that come to mind.

Visit The Inn and walk hand in hand with Payton as she heals and seeks to restore true love.

Get your copy of this clean romantic beach read today!

Pelican Beach Series:
> **The Inn at Pelican Beach: Book 1**
> **Sunsets at Pelican Beach: Book 2**
> **A Pelican Beach Affair: Book 3**
> **Christmas at Pelican Beach: Book 4**
> **Sunrise At Pelican Beach: Book 5**

Printed in the USA
CPSIA information can be obtained
at www.ICGtesting.com
LVHW010742100724
785084LV00015B/609